Mending Angel's Wings

Based on a True Story

Mending Angel's Wings

By Charity Angel

Published by Charity Angels Creations
2014

First Printing: 2014

ISBN 978-1-312-35401-2

4

Dedicated in gratitude to those who broke my wings, and to those who mended them.

Today God Sent an Angel

Every day God sends down angels to the earth below.
Each has accepted that His plan will help them learn and grow.
Their tasks will not be easy, their journey will feel long.
Through all the trials and the pain, they will learn that they are strong.
Sometimes they will feel that they walk alone and wander down dark paths.
Many times they will feel blessed by doing what God the Father asks.
Each angel has a mission to fulfill that is theirs and theirs alone.
Every one of them will struggle to return to their heavenly home.
Some angel's wings are broken in two, others have become tattered and torn. Some have life experiences that have caused them to deeply mourn.
No matter what paths they take, or the number of steps they trod, each angel is very precious and forever loved by God.
God sends down His angels each and every day. They help, lift, and strengthen one another all along the way.
He knew they all would seek a time and place where the pain finally ended.
He sent His Only Begotten Son so that all broken wings are mended.

Contents

Prologue

Prologue

A sense of absolute resolve began to envelope me. I immediately felt cold and distant as I drew myself inward for protection. My hair began to stand up on the back of my neck, and a thick tension started to suffocate all the air in the room. I instinctively knew something bad was coming.

I began to shake my head in disbelief. I could not believe my ears nor my eyes as I listened to his entire confession. Thoughts of broken trust, years of betrayal and all the lies of the last four years filled my mind.

Suddenly, I grew a backbone of ice cold steel. I glared as I faced him and stood totally erect. I looked him straight in the eyes with a dagger like stare, and said in a very low and firm tone, "Give it to him yourself!"

I raised my right hand with my arm fully extended and my palm firmly facing him. "I'm done!" I stated, as I whirled around and calmly walked back down the hall. I quickly grabbed bags for me and my children and began to pack.

Chapter 1

Destiny Will Not Wait

I took one step out the door and immediately the cold wind nipped at my cheeks and nose. I glanced upward and saw what looked like cottonwood seeds slowly dancing together joyfully in the sky. I gazed at the world around me and could not help but be amazed by the piles of fluffy whiteness that had fallen during the two hours that I had been indoors.

I walked up to a small fluffy pile that was sitting on the branch of a nearby tree and scooped it up in my glove covered hands. It was not cottonwood seeds at all, but snow. I marveled at each little individual snowflake; how light and airy they each were.

In the 17 years that I had been alive, I had never seen snow look like this. Thousands and thousands of little shapes, all of them different and unique, combined together perfectly to make such purely beautiful looking snow. I smiled to myself as I blew them off my hands like the seeds of a dandelion flower.

The sound of feet scraping the cobblestone path behind me quickly caught my attention. I turned around in time to see my little brother Gabriel playing in the snow. He was clearly as amazed as I was by the unusual snow. He usually did not venture out into the cold because of how much he hated it, but it was clear that he could not help himself.

There was something magical about it all. As I was thinking about this, I felt a tingling inside, and I knew that it was true. Just as my brother decided to go back inside our small stone cottage, I heard a feminine voice.

"Angelica", she whispered. I looked around but saw no one. Again she called to me "Angelica." I could see nothing. If it wasn't for all of the experiences I had before this moment, I would have thought that I was hearing things or that maybe I was a little crazy.

I knew that someone was trying to communicate with me. I closed my eyes and focused on opening my heart. I absorbed all the sounds around me. I invited the energy of nature to move through me, and then I felt her. I felt her standing right next to me.

I opened my eyes, and I beheld her. A beautiful young woman with long brown hair that was as dark as chocolate, yet it also glistened in the sun like it has been kissed with glittering crystals. It was clear that she was not in the same spiritual plane as me, she was beyond the veil.

Sensing that I could now see her she continued, "Angelica, you must not waste any more time here. It is time that you move forward in your life. You must fulfill your purpose. If you delay much longer, you will miss your chance, and all will be lost."

I knew what she was speaking of. I had dreams about it every night for the last 14 years. I looked back at the cottage of my childhood. I thought about my lonely mother, my two little brothers, and four younger sisters. I was saddened by the thought that I must leave them.

My mother left my father years ago. He had remarried and started a new life. We were all that each other had. How could I explain to them that I must leave them now? Anytime I mentioned leaving, I was told that I was the glue in the family, and if I left, everything would fall apart.

Leaving was a moment that I dreaded, but I knew that it must happen, and the time was now. This life adventure is one that everyone must experience at some time in their life. And this was the right time for me.

I slowly walked into our cottage, walked past the hearth that was warmed by the crackling fire and slipped into my bedroom, closing the hand-carved wooden door behind me. I pulled out a small gray wool bag and began to put all of my trinkets and herbs in it.

I found my traveling cloak, and put some extra clothes in as well. I added the silver hairbrush my mother gave me, and the last gift my father gave me, a necklace. I took a moment to reflect on the fact that over the last 14 years, I had only seen my father a handful of times.

I tossed in my journal, a picture I painted of my family, dried fruit and some dried meat. I pulled the drawstring tightly and tied it. I put my deep purple velvet cloak on, and stepped into the main room of the house.

My mother looked up from her needle work and my brother Blaze gazed up from his book at the same moment. Before I could say a word my mother spoke.

"Angelica, I know that it is time for you to go. I have known for a while. I have been waiting to see when you would embrace your destiny. You are almost of age. It is time."

I was shocked that my mother already knew, and it seemed that she understood and accepted that this was my time to experience all that life had to offer. My brother looked very confused. I looked at him and said, "Dearest Blaze, I must go now. There are things that I must do; important things. That is the only reason that I would ever leave you, mother and everyone else."

His eyes swelled up with tears, and my heart ached more as each one trickled down his cheeks. I rushed to him and held him close. I held the back of his head with my right hand, and I dropped my bag as I embraced him with my other arm. "It will be alright," I said. "You will see," as I stroked his hair gently.

My mother smiled knowingly at me. She embraced Blaze and me together. As I picked up my bag and turned to head out the door I took one last look at all my sisters sitting around the table. They were so young that they seemed unaware that I was preparing to leave.

My mother said, "Angelica, this is the moment that you will truly discover who you really are. Do not be afraid to be open and willing to go where ever your heart takes you. Many before you have wrestled with their own paths of self-discovery. Do not hide who you are my dear. Don't deny your own truth."

Tears began to fill my eyes. I tried to suppress them, while at the same time unknowingly ignoring the counsel that she had just given me. One single tear escaped down my left cheek. I opened the door, and the cold once again nipped at my cheeks and nose. I took that first step forward; that first step that would change everything.

Chapter 2

It is About the Journey

My journey started out slow and I knew that I was leaving everything I knew behind. I thought about our village, and how simple it was compared to the other villages that I had heard about. Everyone here, and in some of the surrounding villages, had chosen to live a very simple life.

Some villagers travelled using horses and wagons, while those in our village still travelled on foot. We determined to not get swept up in all the modern things that some of the other villages were. Part of me loved the simple life I had lived, but there was also a spark of desire to learn and experience new things.

Suddenly my thoughts were interrupted. "Angelica," a still small voice whispered. "Yes," I replied. "Angelica, my name is Comfort. I am your spirit guide. Everyone has been given a guide to help them through this life. I have been with you since birth. I will remain your guide while you are in mortality. I have been sent by the Creator. He has given you many wonderful spiritual gifts. I am here to help you develop them."

Comfort continued, "These gifts are subject to natural law. You must use them to fulfill the purposes of the Creator. They are to never be used to prosper you personally. You are to only use them for good, never misuse them.

Any time that you begin to use them for selfish reasons, they will weaken and you will no longer be able to access them at will. You must remember to listen to me as your guide in order to remain safe and protected as well as to be able to access these gifts fully."

I stopped in the middle of the path and turned to Comfort and said, "When you say spiritual gifts, do you mean the dreams that I have?" Comfort replied, "That is just one of your many gifts. There are more to come. More that you need to develop."

I thought about this as I continued down the path. "Where are we going?" I asked. Comfort replied, "Angelica, you already know. As you continue down this road, you will see the things that will remind you of some of the places and experiences from your dreams. You will know where to go and when, as long as you remain true to yourself, the Creator, and the gifts that are within you.

Any time that you deny your gifts or ignore them, you will have to find your way back to the path. I am here to guide, warn, protect and comfort you, but you will always be able to choose for yourself whether or not to listen to me. You do not have to listen to me or follow the Creator if you do not want to. However, there are consequences to your choices, and you do not get to choose what those are."

I pondered on this for quite some time. To me, it seemed like a great gift to be able to choose for myself. At the same time, it seemed a little scary to not be able to choose what would happen whenever I made a choice. I suddenly realized that this applied to both the good and bad choices that I made each and every moment of my life.

As I continued to walk down the path through the forest. I could not help but wonder how long it would be before I saw the meadow; the one that I had seen in my dreams over and over again. In my dreams, it was my favorite place to be. It delighted all of my senses, and I longed to find a place like that to live forever.

While thinking that I would probably have to walk for days on end and watch the seasons change before I would see the meadow as it was in my dreams, I heard them. I heard the familiar sound of the birds in the distance.

Suddenly, without warning, the snow stopped falling and a hush fell over the forest. The forest became thick and lush and it was then that I noticed the aspen and evergreen trees.

The shimmering glorious sun was dancing jubilantly in and out of the branches. It was clear that it was enjoying filling the day and the land with light. A moist fog spiraled along the edges of the trees. I instinctively knew what was coming. My heart filled with warmth and joy when I saw it.　Down in a small valley below where I was standing, was the meadow.

The vaporous mist rolled like a wave towards the center of the meadow from the forest floor in the gentle breeze. The sun kissed the grass and flowers while the dew raced to escape its rays. Birds were singing their morning greetings to each other. Their chirruping continued to increase in volume until it was almost the only sound that could be heard.

As I reached the edge of the dense forest, I watched the birds float in and out of the edge of it and flutter to a tree in the center of the meadow. I smelled the reassuring and familiar scent of lilac and lavender in the warm breeze.

My mind wrestled with the idea that this beautiful place from my dreams was real. My dreams and reality became indistinguishable at that moment. Instinctively, I knew what I needed to do. I descended into the meadow and began walking through a plethora of wild flowers. As I strolled forward, I ran my fingers through some of them in order to convince my mind and body to accept that all of this was truly real.

I enjoyed hearing the whipping sound of my long skirt brushing against my ankles and the soft, grass covered soil. I slipped off my shoes for a moment, and enjoyed the feeling of gently curling my toes in the loamy soil. I relished in the texture and all the sensations I was experiencing.

Every one of my senses was telling me that this was real. I turned my gaze to the solitary tree in the middle of the meadow. I became fixated with it. It sat slightly up on a hill of bright green grass, just as I remembered it.

I picked up my shoes in one hand. It was then that I noticed deer, rabbits and other woodland creatures gravitating towards the tree. After a few moments of watching them, I felt an inner desire, almost a beckoning, that I should walk to the tree too.

As I approached the tree, I placed my right hand upon its trunk and let my shoes drop from my other hand. My shoes landed almost silently in the grass. I took in all the sights and sounds around me. My senses became clearer and I acknowledged the smell of wild daisies and sunflowers.

I became aware of shimmering drops of dew on the grass. I felt the joy of the bees and butterflies as they hopped and skipped from flower to flower. I turned my gaze upwards. Beautiful hues of blue, pink and orange filled the sky.

The sun had almost finished rising. As I looked upward through the branches, I noticed the crisscrossing patterns that they formed. I relaxed almost immediately the moment I saw the leaves trembled in the breeze. Here, everything was as it should be. It was perfect, and I recognized that I felt at peace.

After some time, Comfort's voice interrupted my thoughts and drew me into the present. "Angelica, this is a place of rejuvenation that the Creator has made for each and every one of us. It is not a place that you can stay in forever yet. You must try to remember this place when things get tough, when you are struggling. Carry this feeling of the Creator's love for all things inside of you always. It will provide you the peace and strength that you need. If you can do this, you will be able to withstand more than even you can fathom right now."

"I love this place; I never want to leave it," I thought. I knew that staying here really was not possible with all that I needed to do. Full of regret, I bowed my head and I removed my hand from the tree. Slowly, I slipped my shoes back on.

I closed my eyes and stretched out my hands to my sides and raised them slightly. I encouraged myself to sense and feel everything around me. I absorbed all the positive energy I could and felt overjoyed with all of the life and beauty that surrounded me.

I looked toward Comfort and said, "Will I really be able to accomplish all that I have been shown in my dreams? Will I really find who I am looking for? Will it all turn out good in the end?" Comfort replied, "It is not yet determined. For you have the ability to choose for yourself. It is possible that you may choose to take another course. If that is the case, then a new outcome must come to pass. What that will be, I do not know. However, the Creator knows. He knows you, he knows your thoughts, the desires of your heart, and he knows the path you will take."

I shuddered at the thought of what life would be like if I did not make the right decisions. If I didn't find what my life's purpose is. If I never found the perfect man for me.

One thing that I understood completely was that I would not be able to find my companion and stand beside him until I was willing to strive to reach my full potential. I must become who I am meant to be in order to even have the ability to find him. I must accept who I really am.

The thought of failure became overwhelming, but the feeling of the victory that could await me was stronger. Deep down I knew I would fight for him; for this man that I never met; a man who would be my equal in all things.

"It is time to move forward Angelica." Comfort said firmly. I longingly took one last look at the meadow then averted my eyes toward the west. The darkness of the road ahead scared me. I felt no desire to travel it, but I knew that I had to. I knew that I must go into the heart of these woods of life in order to find my true self. I must learn many different types of lessons. Through these experiences I knew I would develop the ability to confidently embrace all that I am.

As I approached the edge of the woods, I heard the cries of others who had wandered into them that were lost. I had been taught about the many different paths that people can stumble upon in these woods. They can become sad, burdened, and so lost that they never come back.

For just a moment, I worried that I may spend my entire life in there as well, lost like they were, sad like they were. "I will be with you." Comfort said. And with that, I took the first step into the darkness.

Chapter 3

One Step at a Time

Once I had placed both my feet on this new path, I stood there for a moment waiting for my eyes to adjust. It did not take long before I began to see the long crippled finger-like branches of nearby trees reaching out into the thick and heavy darkness.

The longer I stood in the darkness, the more my vision cleared and I was able to see all that surrounded me. I felt scared and confused. I questioned, "How can I see so clearly now when it was so dark before?" Comfort whispered, "Everyone eventually becomes accustomed to the level of light that they are standing in." While I felt some comfort from being given this knowledge, I also felt very uneasy.

Deep inside I knew that no matter what the circumstances were, I did not want to become accustomed to the darkness. I found myself immediately longing for the light. I desperately yearned to be back in it. I desired the peace of the meadow, and the companionship of the sun and all the woodland creatures.

However, I also knew that this journey was meant to be taken. I was meant to be here; to go through all that still lie ahead. I instinctively knew that it was for my own good, so that I would be able to learn and grow, find myself, and fulfill my life's purpose. This journey was authored by a Divine Creator, who knew that the best way for me to discover who I am, was to be confronted with choices, trials, and temptations.

My inner voice confessed to me that what lay ahead could be horrible, it could be incredibly difficult, scary and intense. It was possible that at times I would question if I could make it through it. My inner voice reassured me and declared the reality of the fact that there was no other way.

I was pulled from my thoughts by the cries of other voices. I knew that these were the cries from the disembodied, forever lost. Some sounded like they felt abandoned and alone. There was a part of me that wanted to rush to their aid. I was torn on the inside every time I heard them crying. I did not know what to do.

I was searching for my purpose, and I had no idea what it was. I had no direction. I questioned, "What am I supposed to do?" Comfort whispered, "Look inside yourself, connect with the Creator."

I clasped my hands together interlocking my fingers and pulled them to my chest. I turned my thoughts inward. I waited for a feeling of connection to rise. Once it was there, I asked the Creator what to do. The answer came, "Keep walking, it is not safe here." I realized that somehow my inner voice knew more than I did. She was connected to a higher source. She could sense things I did not notice on my own. I determined to listen to her.

As I moved forward, I hesitated before taking each step. I waited for reassurance to come that I should continue to walk in the direction I was. Eventually, I became comfortable with the path, and I followed it without any more hesitation.

I began to notice how different this place was from anything else that I had ever seen. I had heard rumors about the woods, but that is all I knew, rumors. As I continued to walk along the clearly defined path, I began to appreciate the trees, the overcast sky, and the moon.

There was something about this place that made me feel joyous and adventurous. I felt that whatever my purpose was, I was sure to discover it. Nothing was going to stand in my way, I was going to be successful in this journey.

There was no one else who knows for sure what my purpose is, except the Creator, and he had not revealed it to me. Whenever I would inquire about my life, I would be told, "Be still, I will give you a little at a time as you need it."

This was frustrating of course, because I wanted to know the end from the beginning. I wanted to know where I was supposed to end up, what I was supposed to do. I realized that I would have to learn to trust myself, the Creator's plan and trust that I would understand each new bit of information that I was given.

I felt that I was trying to plot a course while being blind. I could not see what was ahead, or where I was supposed to end up. I decided that I would just have to make sure I made it through each moment, wherever I was on the path.

I was pulled from my thoughts by movement in the distance. I saw what looked like the shape of a person, sitting quietly on a log beside the path just ahead of me. I panicked with the thought that this would be the first human contact that I had since I left my family. I felt uncertain about walking past whoever it was. I thought, "Maybe this is the man I have been looking for?" My inner voice pressed me to keep going, to just ignore the figure on the log.

Chapter 4

Trust the Inner Voice

As I got closer to the mysterious figure, I realized that it was a young man. He was attractive. He had light brown hair with blonde highlights. His lightly tanned skin made his greenish blue eyes stand out in an almost penetrating way. I had never seen such a good looking young man before.

I sensed danger. My inner voice told me to avoid him. My eyes told me he was harmless. I did not understand why I was having mixed thoughts and feelings. How could someone so pleasing to look at be a danger to me?

He looked up, and smiled at me as he said, "Hello." "Hi," I replied shyly. He stood up turning completely around to face me. He was about my same height, just a little taller. He came close enough to me that I could tell that he smelled really nice. He had a kind of spicy, musky smell. He looked me in the eye and said, "Can I join you on your walk?" Shocked that I was getting so much attention from him, I nodded my head yes.

He quickly grabbed a large burlap bag overflowing with apples that was sitting beside the log where he sat just moments before, and lifted a small pack onto his back. I was amazed at the physical strength that he had. The feeling that I was in danger persisted, but my focus fixated on his every move and my attraction to him. I ignored all other feelings.

Comfort whispered, "Get away from him." I became irritated by her words. I felt like they were stiff bristles being brushed against my soft skin. We were just walking together. I was fine. I felt a feeling of caution rise, I suppressed it; I knew I was not going to stay with him forever.

As we walked, we talked about his life. "My father left when I was young." He said with a deep sadness in his voice. "My mother remarried, and they had a son together. I felt that they loved him more than me, so I left." I felt a kinship to him immediately because our pasts were similar.

"You are so beautiful." He said. I blushed as I replied, "So are you." We both laughed, as we became aware of the fact that I had just called him beautiful. I began to tell him about my family, where I was going, and what I was hoping to find. He smiled, and we found a lot to talk about that made us laugh.

Without warning, he reached out and took my hand in his. It took my breath away. My stomach flittered and fluttered. He started running down the path, and I completely enjoyed the feeling of running with him.

Once we reached a clearing, we sat down to eat. He gave me one of his yellow apples that looked as though they had been kissed with a little red blush on the top. As I took a bite out of it, the flesh was crisp and I felt intense pleasure from the sweet juices as they rushed into my mouth and wrapped around my teeth and tongue.

I reached into my bag and offered him some of the dry meat that I had brought with me. As we ate, I realized that I did not even know his name. I finished eating my dried meat, and I said, "My name is Angelica." He smiled then said, "Hi Angelica. My name is Damien."

As he said his name, I felt hair rise up on the back of my neck and forearms, the sensation of being in danger returned. Again, I chose to ignore it. After all, I enjoyed having someone to talk to, he was cute, and he hadn't done anything that I should really be afraid of. I told myself I was just being paranoid.

Unexpectedly, Damien laid his head down on my lap and smiled as he looked up at me. I blushed again, and felt a little uneasy with a guy so close to me. I was unsure what to do. I tried to hide the fear that was starting to build up inside of me.

Comfort whispered intensely, "Leave him now." I pretended that I did not hear her. It was getting dark, and the moon was getting higher in the sky. It was clear that if we were going to get any sleep that we would need to get it now.

I rolled my bag up to rest my head on it, and I adjusted my cloak. I felt a little chill. Damien started a fire. The crackling and hypnotizing warmth of the flames had me sleeping in no time.

The sound of chirping filled the air, I opened my eyes. "It must be morning," I thought. Damien had some meat on the fire, and he had sliced up some of his apples. He offered me a little bit of both, which I gladly accepted. I was not certain what kind of meat it was, but it tasted better than anything that I had ever tasted. I thoroughly enjoyed its crisp exterior and soft and tender interior.

I was taken off guard by a sudden nagging feeling that I was in danger and that I needed to leave. I realized that I had not heard Comfort speak one word to me since I ignored her the night before.

I slowly started to get up. I grabbed my bag, and I prepared to leave. Damien asked "Are you planning on going on alone?" "Yes," I said. He said, "There really is no reason to do that. I want to go with you."

I felt an urgent impression that I should go on alone. My inner voice screamed not to let him walk another step with me. I began to worry that I could offend him. After all, we just spent the entire day and night together. I began to discredit what I was feeling. I thought, he made me laugh, there is no evidence that I was truly in danger.

My desire not to offend him suddenly carried more weight than my desire to listen to my inner voice. Betraying my own intuition, I said, "That would be great. I enjoy being with you." He smiled slyly as he started to put out the fire and prepare for the journey that lay ahead.

I admired how swiftly he worked, and how efficient he was. He had everything cleaned up and was ready to go in no time. It looked as if we had never been there at all.

We continued on the path for several hours. The brush became thicker, and thorny plants started to appear along the path. I was taken by surprise as one of the plants seemed to reach out and slash at my ankles with its thorns.

In contrast, Damien seemed to be very familiar with the area, and he appeared to walk easily through the path unscathed by the thorns. My ankles hurt badly, and they quickly became swollen. We reached another clearing and Damien suddenly stopped.

Damien took a look at my ankles, "That looks like it really hurts. I need to prepare a poultice to take care of them." I sat on a nearby log to wait as he went to gather supplies. I enjoyed feeling the rough texture of the log with my fingertips. I tried to focus on each little crevice in order to avoid and suppress the pain in my ankles.

I took my hair brush out of my bag and brushed my hair a few times trying to deny the situation I was in. As I placed it back in my bag, I took a moment to look at my locket that my father had given me the last time that I saw him. A strong feeling of uneasiness came over me once again.

Everything in me screamed that something was wrong, but I did not know what it was. I guessed at what could be wrong, I thought that maybe I should not be alone. I sensed there was something in the woods that was going to jump out and try to hurt me any second.

Just as the feeling reached such a strong intensity that I was almost driven to tears, Damien stepped into the clearing. I did not have the feeling of relief that I expected to have when I saw him.

His arms were full of some common healing herbs and other plants I had never seen before. As he created the poultice, I decided to lie on the ground with my head against the log. After a short while he was back by my side. "Lie still," he commanded gently as he started to apply the mixture of herbs to my ankles.

To my relief, a majority of my pain quickly dissolved. But then, I began to feel very light headed and dizzy. An intense weakness settled over my entire body, and I suddenly felt like I was floating in the air.

I felt sick to my stomach. I attempted to move but I couldn't. I became full of fear. I wanted to scream, but my mouth refused to comply. I was suddenly reminded of a repetitive nightmare I had many times over the years. I would try to scream, to cry out, and even though my mouth was open and I was screaming with my entire soul, no sound made it past my lips. I was forced to suffer in silence.

A cruel, cold smile crossed Damien's face. In that moment, I realized what a huge mistake I had made. I should have listened to Comfort; I should have listened to my inner voice. There was nothing that I could do now.

There was no one to save me, and even if there was, I could not cry out to them. I was alone, and there was nothing I could do to protect myself. I was completely defenseless.

A warm and sorrow-filled tear trickled down my cheek as I realized that whatever was coming was the result of my recent choices. I had ignored every gift that I had been given to protect me. I had been disobedient. I was easily distracted from what I was supposed to be doing. I had been deceived. And now, the consequences were coming.

I had no idea what Damien was after. I thought "Does he want my supplies? Does he want to kill me?" But, he did not move towards my bag or other supplies; instead, he slowly moved his hands in front of my chest. He used his finger to play with my cloak ties, then began to untie my cloak.

Everything within me wanted to fight him, to resist, to do anything to get away from him, but I could not move. I laid there frozen and helpless. In total astonishment I realized that there was nothing I could do to stop him from doing whatever it was that he wanted to do.

My vision became very foggy. I could barely see him anymore. I started to imagine that I was somewhere else. A place where there is a void of darkness, where nothing exists. No feelings, no images, no light, nothing.

He forced me back to the present as he whispered in my ear, "Do you know what a beautiful girl you are? I really can't help myself. I have to have you. A beautiful girl like you, with soft and smooth skin…"

As he spoke, I felt him touch my arms and gently caress my face. He started to kiss me on my lips and with faked tenderness continued whispering, "...such sweet lips and long hair."

He ran his fingers through my hair and then started to remove my cloak. He continued to whisper to me. "I bet that you have even better treasures for me to uncover and enjoy under all these clothes. It must be a burden to have so many layers on."

Never in my life had I wished more to be somewhere else. I was willing to die if that was the only way to escape what was happening to me. My mind raced with questions. "What will he do with me afterwards if he takes that which is most precious to me?" "Will he kill me?" "Can I recover from these herbs and plants that he has given to me?" "How will I ever get through this!?"

I felt a cool breeze lick at my legs and the wet ground below me as Damien removed more layers of my clothing. I felt damp grass straining to wrap itself around my legs. I tried to scoot backwards, to move away from him, but I still could not move. As he climbed on top of my body, it felt like the weight of the world came crushing down on me. I became filled with even more terror.

My mind raced back to a time when I was a child, after my mother left my father. I remembered being molested by an older boy in my village, and I feared that what was about to happen to me would be much worse. I began crying out to the Creator in my mind. "Oh God! Help me please! Save me!"

Then something miraculous happened. A force I could not see lifted Damien off of my body and flipped him over my head into the thorny bushes. I heard him scream in agony. I did not see or sense anyone or anything that could have possibly thrown him off me. I was scared and confused but at the same time very grateful.

I wondered if somehow I had gained enough strength to throw him off of me, but I knew that I still couldn't move. Whatever happened had saved me from losing what was most dear to me.

I heard the sound of Damien's heavy footsteps as he rapidly ran off into the distance. I closed my eyes in hopes that the effects of the poultice would wear off. I hoped that I would never see Damien again.

Chapter 5

Stumble and Fall

It was morning once again. My body ached as I became more and more conscious of everything around me. I realized that I had slept an entire day. I struggled to move. I discovered that I could wiggle my toes and finger tips. Slowly, I regained control of my entire body.

If it was not for my inability to move, I would have thought that Damien was just a bad dream. Part of me wanted it to be. I did not want to believe that something so horrible had happened to me. I cried and tried to console myself over and over again as I gathered all of my things and headed back towards the path.

The more I wandered, the more that I felt that I was not going to find my way back. I was disoriented and completely unsure of myself. I questioned every move that I made. I started to tell myself that I was stupid. That no one else would have been as dumb as I was. They would have listened to their inner voice and the voice of their spirit guide.

The more that I thought negative thoughts about myself, the more negative voices seemed to fill my head. Eventually, it felt like I had an entire crowd ridiculing me, mocking me and putting me down. As these voices increased, my inner voice was very hard to hear. The more I walked, the more these voices tormented me.

They told me that I was dirty, not good enough and that I would never succeed. They told me that I would not find the man in my dreams now because I had disobeyed. I was forever lost to the Creator, and he would have nothing to do with me anymore.

Overtime, I started to believe that what they said was true. I started to think that I would never succeed and that I would be forever lost in these dark woods.

I would never see my family again. It was at this point that I found a glass like pond. It was quiet and still all around it. I determined that if I was never going to find the path again, that I would live out the remainder of my life here in this calm, safe and peaceful place.

In the distance, I heard rustling in the bushes. I froze, afraid of what could be there. A girl with coal black hair and dark piercing eyes stepped out from behind a large leafy bush. She smiled at me. "I'm Jessica," she said as she started to dust herself off.

It did not take long for us to become friends. I had felt so alone that I welcomed her presence. We spent many days together collecting berries and nuts. Jessica taught me about roots and other foods that I could eat that I had never tried before.

She was very good at making me laugh. And that is what we did most of the time, laugh and tease each other and have fun. But one day, that all changed. We were walking down a dirt path, when in the distance I could see Damien. He was running and laughing with a girl, and tackling her to the ground. The moment I saw him, I collapsed to the ground.

Suddenly, I heard loud sob-filled screaming. It shook me to the very core of my being. Jessica reached out touching my shoulder and in a concerned and terrified voice said, "Angelica, what is wrong?" In that moment, I became aware of the fact that the screaming was coming from me.

Jessica looked over the same direction that I was, and instinctively knew that she had to get me to safety. She hurried and pulled me off the path before Damien or anyone else could see me. Once I calmed down, she asked me what happened. I told her everything.

"That is horrible," she said understandingly. "Why did you not tell me before?" "I was embarrassed and ashamed." I replied. "I should have listened to my impressions." "That does not make it your fault. It was not right. You should tell the protective council." Jessica said sternly. I did not want to tell anyone else, and I was determined not to talk about it ever again.

As I was gathering wood to build a permanent shelter for Jessica and me, I came across a path that led to a stretch of land that was still cold and covered with ice. While I was exploring the area I noticed a small cottage.

It was made of rough hand-hewn stone. Its wood shutters and large wood door were warm and inviting. Afraid to talk to other people anymore, I turned away quickly and headed back towards my safe and secluded pond that Jessica and I shared.

I heard the door of the small cottage open, I turned around and was greeted by a smiling young man. He was tall with very dark hair and blue eyes. There was a sparkle in his eyes. He asked me if I wanted something to eat. My lips flattened as I clinched my mouth shut tighter. I looked at the ground and started to back away.

He said, "Hold on. I can tell that you are scared. I do not want to hurt you. I will just put some food on a plate and leave it on that rock over there under the big tree," as he pointed towards it. I looked toward where he pointed, and he continued, "I will go back inside and then you can go and get it."

I nodded my head in agreement, as I walked far off to wait for him to do what he said he would. I had stopped believing any of the words that people said to me, and waited to see the evidence that what they said was true.

After he left, I went up to the rock and started to eat. It had been a very long time since I had a warm meal. I was able to enjoy fresh fruit and crunchy vegetables that grew naturally in the forest. I had not brought any weapons or tools to prepare any other types of food.

Over the next few weeks, the young man continued to leave plates of food for me whenever I ventured away from Jessica on my own. I enjoyed the food a lot. It made me feel cared for, and over time, I felt a sense of happiness and fulfillment. The food started to provide a level of security. I came to rely on it every day.

One day, he approached me while I was eating. "I believe that it is time that we get to know each other," he said firmly. He told me that his name was Anthony. Each day I came to eat, he would come out and talk with me. Eventually he convinced me to come into his cottage and enjoy my meals there.

I enjoyed many nights by his fire and we had discussions that lasted long into the night. I began to gain the courage to trust him. Eventually I told him all about Damien, my family and the life that I knew before meeting him.

I did not tell him about Comfort, finding the purpose in my journey or any of the thoughts that I had been having the last several weeks. I kept those negative thoughts inside. Whenever they tried to come near the surface, I would bury them alive once again.

Eventually we grew very close. I felt attracted to him, but I knew that he was not the man in my dreams, and I did not want to be more than friends. After a while, I brought him to my cottage by the pond. He came every night in order to help me feel safe and protected.

At first he slept outside, but after a while Jessica and I worried about Anthony getting too cold, so we invited him to sleep on the floor in front of the fire. After all, we reasoned, if someone did come to hurt us, he was in the best place to protect us.

After some time, he tried to kiss me. Out of curiosity, I let him, just to see what it felt like to kiss someone without being drugged and nearly unconscious. Kissing him did not change how I felt about him like I hoped it would. It did not change how I felt about myself. But, it did feel good, and it brought me some temporary relief from the pain I felt inside.

After some time, Anthony convinced me to go and talk to the protective council of the forest about what happened with Damien. Because so much time had passed, they had a very hard time believing me. Some of the members of the council tried to tell me that I was lying, and that I made it up. Others told me that Damien told them that I did everything willingly and just felt guilty now.
I regretted ever telling any of them about what had happened. It only made me feel worse. It felt like there were a hundred eyes staring at me in judgment. It was overwhelming.

Anthony tried to comfort me by telling me that he believed me. He said that he knew that it happened, and that I was telling the truth. He felt bad about the way that the council acted. Sometimes we would come across other people as we were traveling between my cottage and his. Many of them would mock me and say hurtful things because the news of what I told the council had spread throughout that part of the forest.

One day I was alone in a field of wildflowers. A small brown rabbit hopped up to where I was sitting. His long brown floppy ears made me smile. The moment that I touched his soft coat to pet him, I heard a voice, "Angelica, what happened was not your fault. You made the best decisions you could have with the knowledge and experience that you had at the time."

I was grateful for the kind words from this woodland creature. They gave me just enough strength to keep on going. I decided that it did not matter what people thought. I knew the truth, the Creator knew the truth, and he had saved me.

I knew that Anthony was not the man that I was trying to find. Even though I told him that I did not want to spend the rest of my life with him, he did not seem to take me seriously. He continued to try to move the relationship forward towards marriage.

One day after I had been out gathering food in the forest, I came back to the cottage to the sound of Anthony screaming. I dropped everything and ran in the door. I was shocked to discover that Jessica had taken her shirt off and was trying to seduce Anthony.

"Jessica!" I screamed. "I cannot believe that you would do this to me! I thought that you were my friend!" "Angelica, it is not what it looks like. It was an accident." "I am not stupid," I said. "I want you out! Get out of here!" Within a few moments Jessica gathered up all of her things and ran out the door.

I was heartbroken that someone that I had trusted to live with me had hurt me. I questioned if I would ever be able to have close friends, especially girlfriends. I had never experienced this type of betrayal before. I regretted that I had shared as much as I did with Jessica.

Several days later, I told Anthony that I wanted to be alone. "Anthony, I really don't want to have anyone in my life anymore. The other night when I told you that I did not want to be more than friends, I was serious." Anthony looked at me with his deep blue eyes, and simply responded, "Ok."

I felt very awkward telling Anthony the truth about not wanting to be more than friends, so I decided to pick wild flowers in a nearby field in order to clear my mind. Over the last several months, I went to the meadow when I was feeling lost, alone or confused. I would often reflect on the meadow that I left behind. I longed to be there again, and to feel that love, peace and wholeness once more.

My inner voice whispered, "Angelica, don't go to the meadow today." I wanted to get away from everything for a while, and I figured that there would be no harm in going to the meadow, so I disobeyed my inner voice. I walked into the meadow anyway.

While reaching for some beautiful red-orange Indian Paint Brush, I heard some unfamiliar sounds. There was crackling and snapping in the distance. As it intensified in volume, I turned to see what it was and where it was coming from.

The moment I turned my head I could clearly see a log swinging towards me from one of the nearby trees. I was terrified, and I tried to duck to avoid it. I knew that I had failed the second that it hit me in the back, knocking me to the ground.

My neck was slammed into the ground and was brought to a sudden halt against a rough and gnarled tree root. Intense burning spread across my neck and down my right shoulder. The wound began to sting simultaneously. My back hurt terribly. Hot, salty tears streamed down my cheeks as I laid weakly on the dark and cold damp earth.

A feeling of dizziness consumed me completely. I knew that I could not stand up on my own. I felt frightened. "This is just like how I felt when Damien drugged me," I thought to myself.

Just then Anthony appeared. "What happened?" he cried. I tried to explain to him what had happened, but I could not.

My words were jumbled together. It was clear that I had a concussion. I continued to try to form words to express all I was thinking and feeling, but they would not come out clearly. Anthony placed one of his fingers over my lips and said, "Hush now. Don't try to speak. It will all be alright."

"I'm going to take care of you. I'll take you back to my cottage, and I will do whatever I need to for you to recover." He said soothingly as he wrapped his strong arms around me and lifted me up from the ground.

I felt my clothing cling to me everywhere the moisture from the ground had gotten through it. Anthony used his chin to brush hair out of my face, and gently kissed my forehead. Feeling his strong hands around my shoulder and his arm under my legs, I felt at peace and relaxed.

I drifted in and out of consciousness. I saw Anthony's face again as I heard the sound of the cottage door opening. I tried to focus on the details of his face, particularly his eyes, but I could not get my vision to become clear enough.

I saw the ceiling of his cottage. I tried to focus my eyes again. I could barely see the outline of his face, and then I felt soft fur beneath me. "Why am I not wearing any clothes?" I questioned as my eyes rolled back into my head.

When I became conscious again, I thought, "Maybe more has happened to me than just getting hit in the head. He must have had a reason to wrap me in fur like he has. Is this a dream?" I struggled to connect details. I was not sure what was going on. All I could do was feel pain and weakness.

In the middle of the night, I became semi-conscious. This time, I knew for a fact I was naked and cold. I strained to see through the darkness what was going on. My vision was cloudy, but I was certain that I saw Anthony. His shirt was off, and he was starting to lay on top of me. "No," I muttered. "No, I don't want to do this." I fell unconscious once again.

Beautiful and glimmering moonlight streamed through the cottage window. It glistened on the wooden table and chairs. Startled, I realized that I was still naked. Soft and silky furs caressed my back, and using my fingertips to crawl across the blanket that was on me, I realized that it was covered in fur too.

Glancing around quickly, there was no sign of Anthony. I shivered as I questioned, "Was it all a dream?" Maybe it was a flashback of what had happened with Damien, or maybe it was just some crazy sex filled dream that I had because of my concussion.

I continued to look around the room. It was empty and a dark vapor filled the room. There was a feeling of apathy, a type of uncaring that crept through the night air. A dim light from the ashes of the fire flickered in the distance, and smoke climbed slowly up into the air. With a start, I suddenly felt something beside me on the bed, cloaked by the darkness. I gasped and tears began to stream down my cheeks as I realized that it was Anthony. And, he was completely naked.

The moonlight illuminated him clearly. Seeing Anthony lying there sleeping soundly, removed all doubt about the small bits and pieces that I remembered. It became clear that it was not a dream. I continued to sob quietly. Thoughts raced through my mind so fast that I could hardly grasp on to them.

Tears spilled down my cheeks as I contemplated the thought, "I do not love this man." I began to fill with rage as I realized that he had taken what was most sacred to me, my virginity. The violation was just too much to bare.

Confused and angry, I screamed out in my mind to God, "Why!? Why God? Why me? How is it that I was spared this fate before only to have to go through it now?!" Then, a small seed of bitterness was planted deeply in my heart.

Now I have to choose Anthony. No other man would love me now that my virginity was gone. No other man will want me. I felt used. I was completely and utterly devastated. I felt that I was worth less than I was before.

Chapter 6

Believing Lies

Sitting near the edge of a beautiful, pond I looked into the water. I was totally disconnected from the world around me. I knew I was all alone. I felt very confused. I gazed at my reflection in the shimmering glass-like surface of the water.

At first, my eyes were drawn to the rays of the sun as it danced and jumped across the rippled reflection of the sky. Little bursts of light quickly twinkled, then vanished. Then I began to notice my reflection. I was shocked and dismayed at how clear and happy it looked. I looked deep into my eyes.

They shone brightly like two little stars in the darkness. "You are such a liar!" I sneered at myself. "How can you look like that and feel like you do?" I glared at my reflection in the water, then continued. "You have got to come to terms with the fact that you are never going to be the same again!"

My heart swelled in pain as I realized that I did not feel whole anymore. That there was this growing dark and empty space that was beginning to swallow up my joy and hope like a big swirling black hole.

"There will never be another man that will choose me under these circumstances." I thought as I collapsed to the ground in a heap. It was then that I determined that I must accept and succumbed to my fate.

It had been three weeks since Anthony took advantage of my accident. For three weeks I knew that my journey was thwarted once and for all. I was not going to ever find the man that I had been looking for. I was in deep despair, and I felt that I would never recover. I did not want this. I did not want him. I wanted out.

I continued to look deep into the pond. I focused on the thick and slimy murkiness that floated across the bottom of it. I wished that I could just slip into it. I wanted to sink as low as I could, disappear under the warm water, and never be heard from or seen by anyone ever again.

Along with that thought, came the thought of my mother, my brothers, and my sisters. I did not want to leave them. I did not want to return to them a failure.

I slapped my reflection in the water, and growled to myself. "I hate you!" I screamed out loud. "You are too trusting! Too naïve and gullible! This is all your fault!"

Tears began to roll out of the corners of my eyes slowly, one single tear at a time. It was as if each tear did not want to be released, each one clung on until the last possible moment.

Suddenly a beautiful golden brown deer stepped out of the woods and came into my view. He seemed to float just above the water's edge. I realized that he was coming straight for me. My breath caught in my throat, afraid that I might startle it if I made a single sound.

The deer walked up to me and placed its head gently against my forehead. He nuzzled my right cheek, and I thoroughly enjoyed the velvety texture of his fur. Then, I heard a masculine voice. "Angelica, you are not really trapped. You are free to go, if that is what you choose to do."

I was taken off guard. Was this my inner voice? No, it couldn't be. My inner voice was female. I recognized, that somehow the presence of the deer helped me to connect with this masculine guide.

I questioned if I could trust this new voice, or this experience at all. With all that I had been through, I felt that I could not trust myself or my judgment. I continued to ponder on whether or not the message from the deer was true. As I did this, he suddenly pulled away and bounded back into the forest.

Without another thought, I stood up, gathered my things, and walked away. I had no idea where I was going or what I was doing. I just walked. I walked as far as I could, as fast as I could. Eventually I became exhausted and I stopped to rest for the night.

I was awoken by a stream of dancing moonlight that had flickered back and forth then came to rest upon my face. I sensed that I wasn't alone. Like a whisper in the darkness, I heard Comfort's voice. "Hello Beloved Angelica." I was suddenly filled with a feeling of great love. And my heart swelled. I refused to allow myself to feel too much emotion, so I suppressed my feelings of joy. "That was the best choice you could have made." Comfort continued. "You are far from the path now. You need to return to it."

I struggled with the truth of her words. I had no idea how I was going to get back to the path. I became filled with guilt at the realization that I was not the same person who had started on this journey. I concluded therefore, that I was not who I was supposed to be. I felt even more tarnished and worn down than I had before.

"Comfort," I whispered, "I am tired. I have no idea how to right all that is wrong. I am sorry that I did not listen to you." Comfort replied, "That is the perfect place to start." I drifted back into a deep restful sleep.

When I arose in the morning, I was determined to find my way back to the path. I gathered my things together, pausing for a moment to put on the necklace that my father gave me. I felt a renewed strength as I told myself that he loved me.

I continued walking for days until I came to a very high mountain. The terrain looked perilous. Something inside me whispered, "Angelica, this is the only way back."

I started up the mountain. It was not long before I found it hard to breathe. I struggled each day to climb higher, and each day I was rewarded with tasty herbs and the sight of beautiful flowers. As the path became steeper, I would slide back down and become covered in dust. Part of me felt a deep satisfaction each time I overcame a difficult obstacle.

Wild blueberries and raspberries bushes sprinkled along the sides of the trail. They were an especially sweet treat whenever I stopped to rest. I would often gather more than I needed and dry them in the sun so that I could carry them with me.

Climbing higher than I ever had before, I began to hear laughter in the distance. I felt nervous, but I had a strong desire, a compulsion to be around other people. I continued to climb higher and higher until it sounded like the laughter was just around the corner.

I slowly placed my hands on the rough stone in front of me and peered around the bend. Below I saw a wide open field. In the very center of the field was an entire village full of people. There were many huts that were gathered together in clusters, as well as several that littered the distance that seemed to stand strangely alone. "I have never seen so many people in one place in my entire life," I thought to myself.

Everywhere I looked, everyone seemed to have bright and cheerful smiles on their faces. "How can so many people all be happy at the same time?" I wondered. Curious, I cautiously began the trek down into the field in the valley.

As I got closer to the center of town, I passed by several huts. Each one had a different design. They were unique, and they seem to serve many different purposes. A large hut that had an even larger grass thatched pavilion attached to it captured my attention. It was filled with students that were reading and discussing the contents of golden books. There were other students that were gathered together outside this hut playing a variety of games together.

In the distance I saw several young men tossing a ball back and forth. They laughed whenever someone would score a point. Their buoyant laughter filled my heart with joy.

The people who were playing games seemed so carefree. "I bet that they have never had to go through anything like I have." I thought to myself. It was hard to believe that they had ever experienced anything other than joy in their lives. I desired to be like them.

A peaceful feeling of warmth blanketed the entire village. Not warmth like you would feel from a fire, but a distinct warmness that filled the air and my soul. It was clearly a peaceful place. A safe place. I longed to join in the fun, but I felt uncertain, nervous, and not good enough to join them.

Just then, a young man with sandy blond hair, blue eyes and a full, but crooked smile ran up to me. "Hey!" he yelled. "Hey you! You should join the game! I bet that you could even beat me!" I smiled shyly at him. I had never met someone with such a buoyant personality.

I reluctantly followed him over to where he was playing and took the ball from his out stretched hand. He quickly explained the rules of the game, and then we started to play.

The nervousness began to fade the more that I played. I had never had so much fun in my life. "I win!" I would exclaim each time that I beat him. He would smile at this, and then ask to get another chance to beat me. Each time I won, my confidence grew a little. I loved seeing the smile on his face and the twinkle in his eye. He was so filled with joy that it trickled over into my own soul.

I thought, "Surely this is a guy that would be fun to be around. I would love to get to know him better. I bet that we could be good friends. Maybe even more." The game began to slow down, and we sat next to each other as we watched others take their turn playing. He leaned over to me and said, "I'm Goff." "I'm Angelica." I replied.

Instantly, my mind flashed back to memories of Anthony. I was filled with feelings of guilt, shame and inadequacy. Without even understanding all that I was feeling, or why, I said, "I really need a break." Then I walked over to a spot of grass that was away from everyone. I laid on my back, and gazed up at the clouds.

In the distance I could hear a playful melody being played by a harp. I loved to sing and could not help but be drawn to it. I got up and began to investigate where the joyful noise was coming from. Eventually, I saw a young woman with long blonde hair sitting under a tree. I walked up to her and sat beside her. "Do you know the 'Song of the Heart'?" I asked. She smiled and said, "It is one of my favorites."

"If you play, I will sing it." I said. "Sounds perfect to me," she replied as she started to play. The longer I sang, the better I felt. My sadness drifted away, and for a moment, I felt whole and complete again.

I felt peace, love and joy. I knew that everything was going to be ok. I felt that all was as it should be, and I had no other thoughts or cares in the world. I had forgotten how much I loved singing. I realized how much joy that it made me feel. I wondered, "Why I have not sung a lot more before now?"

After we finished singing and playing together, I had to know who this girl was. "What is your name?" I asked. She responded, "My name is Sherry." "It is nice to meet you Sherry." I said with a smile. I realized that this was the first woman that I had been around in a long time.

"Do you have somewhere to stay?" she inquired. "No," I replied, "I had not even thought about staying here." "You must stay with me!" she exclaimed ecstatically. And with that, she stood up and started walking back towards the village. "Well…" she said questioningly as she motioned for me to follow.

I walked a few steps behind her all the way to a little hut that had a window on each side of the front door. When we walked inside, it radiated a sense of being a warm and cozy place. There were several different colored furs on the floor and the beds that created a patchwork quilt appearance.

There was a log stand that held a hand-carved wood bowl of water for washing her face and hands, and beside it were some of the most beautiful brushes and hair combs that I had ever seen. It had been so long since I had been able to use a washing bowl that I stared at it longingly.

She sensed that I had lacked opportunity to care for myself for a while and said, "Come, we must help you wash up, and I can do your hair." As she combed and braided my hair, I could not help but think about my mother. It had been ages since she had brushed my hair. I truly enjoyed every moment of it.

Once my braid was complete, she had me wash my face and hands using her bowl. She offered some rose scented water for me to put on afterwards. I felt clean and refreshed. It was nice to feel as tender and feminine as a rose.

"We have dinner together in the main hut," she said, as she started towards the door. "It is time to meet there now." When we arrived, I smelled so many different scents of food at once I was overwhelmed.

I felt like I had gone to a land of fantasy that could not possibly be real. I wanted to run up to every table and stuff as many different types of food into my mouth as I could. My stomach rumbled as I wondered how they could have so much when they lived on such a rough and rugged mountain.

Sherry introduced me to many different people. I noticed that many of the women were not happy that I was there. They tried to act nice, but their tone of voice and body language made it clear that they wished that I was somewhere else. The men however seemed to be very excited to meet me.

Many of them came up to me and told me their names. I knew that there was no way that I was going to remember them all. I hoped that Sherry knew who they all were because I was going to need her help if I ever planned to talk to any of them ever again.

One of the outgoing young men approached us as Sherry and I were sitting on a bench together enjoying our food. Just as I looked up at him, he sat down, looked at me and smiled. "Hi." He said. "Hi" I replied looking down.

Just then another young man came over and did the same thing, and then another. I looked at Sherry confused. I had no idea what was going on here. Then one of them said, "I'm Jeremy. Want to go out sometime?" Sherry giggled.

I did not know what to say. As I opened my mouth to respond, each of the other guys asked if I would go out with them. Totally flustered, I replied, "Boys, I'm new here. I am going to need some time." And with that, they smiled and went back to enjoying their food.

After enjoying a great meal, I was relieved when Sherry and I retired to her hut for the evening. Sherry offered to give me some of her old clothes, and some lavender water that I could use whenever I wanted to. As I drifted off to sleep, I smiled to myself. I could not help but feel flattered by all of the attention I was getting. At the same time, I had no idea how to deal with it.

When morning came the smell of freshly fallen rain filled the air. I stepped outside the hut and smiled as I felt sunshine wash across my face. I felt that this village was a good place. I contemplated on whether or not I could live here for a long time.

I decided to walk back to the tree where I had met Sherry, and was interrupted by a young man. "Hi" he said. "Hello" I whispered. He continued, "I noticed that you have been traveling for a long time. I have always wanted to travel. Do you think that you will continue to travel after you stay here awhile?"

I looked at him curiously. I felt a little uncomfortable. I could sense the wheels in his head turning rapidly. He was calculating something, and I was sure that I did not want to know what it was.

I replied, "I may travel again at some time, but right now it is not something that I am thinking about." He smiled, then said "When you decide that you want to travel again let me know. We could marry and travel together."

I looked at him in shock, then thought, "Did he really just say that?!" My mouth fell open. I began to interrogate him, "Is this some kind of joke?" I glared at him as I stated, "I do not find it funny at all. I do not even know you."

He responded, "It is not a joke, I am quite serious. I think that it is better to travel with someone than to travel alone. It seems to me that you are an attractive woman. It would be nice to have the benefits of being married and traveling together. If you find at the end of our travels that you do not want to be my wife anymore, at least we will have enjoyed each other until then."

I stepped to the side of the path that led to the tree and retorted, "There is no way that I would marry you! What kind of arrangement is that?! You must be crazy! Who gets married just to enjoy sex while they travel only to divorce at the end of a trip?! Get away from me!"

He raised his eyebrows in surprise, but smiled as he said "Ok. It was just a thought."

Suddenly Sherry appeared. "Angelica, just ignore him. He is a strange one." And she took me by the hand and led me the rest of the way to the tree. Sherry and I sat by the foot of the tree and talked about everything that we could think of for several hours. We laughed about how forward and crazy that young man had been, and how there was no way that any girl would want to start a relationship with someone like that.

We talked about our dreams. What we hoped our husbands would be like, and what we would want to do when we were getting to know them. Just as we were discussing what things we would not want to do, we heard a commotion in the tall grass.

We became deathly silent as a young man sat up while straightening his tousled hair. He slowly stood up and then walked right up to us and sat down. "I agree with everything you have said." He stated as if he had been part of the conversation all along. Sherry and I looked at each other in surprise. We were both embarrassed that anyone had just heard everything that we had said, but he didn't seem to notice.

He continued to talk on and on about all that he thought, while we just sat back in stunned silence listening. He acted like he knew us both, like we had been friends forever. I started to wonder if he was ever going to shut up, or if he even needed to breathe at all.

Without warning he paused, stuck out his hand towards me and said, "I am Dustin by the way. And you are?" I shook his hand and said, "My name is Angelica, and this is my friend Sherry." At that moment, I heard a voice whisper, "This is your future husband, the father of your children."

I was so terrified at the thought that I jumped up and curtly said, "I have to go!" I ran off towards the village, and I didn't stop until I was able to join those who were playing games completely on the other side of it.

I laughed and played long into the night. I returned to the hut to wash up, and Sherry and I went to dinner. "Wasn't that the strangest thing today with that weird Dustin guy?" I said. "Yeah it was." Sherry replied. "He seemed to just pop up out of nowhere."

"True. I have never seen a guy act that confident." I said. "Do you know him?" "No," Sherry replied. "I don't think that I have ever seen him before, but he does kind of look like this guy who asked me out a long time ago. I turned him down." I thought about this as my mind unwound and I drifted off to sleep.

Several days passed. Each morning I did the same thing. I woke up, ate, washed my face, put on lavender water, walked to the tree with Sherry, sang until the early afternoon, then joined the others playing games until the evening.

Sherry and I ate dinner together, then we went back to her hut and went to sleep. It was a great change from what life had been before. I found myself feeling a little happier every day. I didn't think that I would ever leave this village.

One morning, my consistent schedule was interrupted. I stepped out of the hut to find a bouquet of flowers outside the door. I picked them up and deeply inhaled their pleasant aroma. I noticed a small piece of leather bound to the base of the flowers. On the leather was a note that stated that these flowers were from a young man named Ben.

"Dearest Angelica, it has been a long time since someone has been able to make me smile as much as you do. When I saw these flowers, and how they stood out in the meadow above all the other flowers, I knew that they were meant for you. I do not want to pressure you at all, but I really would like to get to know you. I would like to court you, if you will allow it." I glanced down the note to see that he had signed it "Always Your Friend No Matter What, Ben."

Ben was sweet and told a lot of jokes to everyone gathered to play games. He had a great voice, and many people would ask him to sing their favorite songs all the time. I smiled as I thought about the beautiful gift he had just given me.

Feeling overwhelmed with the increased attention I was getting from several different young men, I continued to reflect on my experiences with Anthony and Damien.

Because those memories had not faded, they tainted my beliefs about men. I was certain that every man was either going to be like they were, or they were going to hurt me in some other way. The thought of being alone with any of them was extremely terrifying to me.

Suddenly Sherry came running up to me and said, "Angelica, Dustin left a note for you." She handed me a piece of leather that was rolled up and tied tightly shut. I opened it and read what it said. "He wants to meet me at the tree" I said.

I had not told Sherry about the voice that I heard that told me he was my future husband. I was scared. I was not sure that I wanted to meet him. I had avoided him for days, and I wanted to keep on avoiding him. "You should at least see what he wants." Sherry said.

I turned and looked up towards the tree its branches were dancing in the breeze. I could see him sitting against the trunk of the tree waiting for me. I looked at my feet and shifted from one foot to the other while brushing them against the dirt. "You will be OK" Sherry said, "I will keep an eye on you from here."

As I approached, Dustin smiled at me. He really looked small and helpless sitting there. In that moment, I felt safe. I felt that if he tried anything, that I would be able to take him down if necessary.

Standing a little ways away from him I questioned, "What do you want?" "I just want to talk with you; get to know you better." He replied. "Why would you want to do that?" I interrogated further. He responded, "Because you seem like a nice girl."

I told him that I was not perfect, and that I had a past. He said that he did not care what my past was, that he was interested in who I am now. I was taken by surprise. This went against everything that I had ever believed about myself.

He must be different. He must be an exception. That intrigued me, and I decided, maybe it was worth taking the time to get to know him after all.

In the weeks that followed, my relationship started to get serious with Dustin. Because of the fact that he accepted all that I told him about me, I felt that I needed to give it a try. I did not really feel attracted to him, and it seemed that we did not have a lot in common.

I believed that if I did not accept his interest in me, that I may never have the chance to get married again.

Part of me didn't want to be too old when I had children. I wanted to be like my mother and grandmother, who both had children when they were young. I did not want to be an old maid, whom no one had wanted when she was in her youth.

He seemed like a safe choice. He was smaller than me, which meant that he was not likely to be able to overpower me. I felt that he was likely to be faithful, because other women were not competing for him.

Once he told me that he had never kissed anyone else, I thought that he would treasure me. I assumed that he found me beautiful. I did not want to feel like I had in the past ever again. I wanted to be stronger than the man that I was with. If I did not take this opportunity now, I may not have another one.

I put all of my plans to continue to travel on hold, and focused on building a relationship with Dustin. In time, he took me to meet his family. They were a bit awkward. The moment I came in the door, it was clear that his parents were offended. When I enquired to what the problem was, Dustin's mother said, "We are not one of those touchy feely families. We don't appreciate hugs, we prefer to keep things formal." I felt very uncomfortable and not very welcomed. Being loving and hugging my family and close friends was natural to me. It was who I had always been.

After dinner, everyone went off in different directions in the house. I was left alone in the guest room. In the distance, I could hear voices. "There must be something wrong with her," his younger brother Harry stated to Dustin's father. "There is no way that someone like that would ever want to be with Dustin." his father replied. "Perhaps he was able to convince her that he is the right guy for her or something." Harry stated in a jealous tone.

I felt sorry for Dustin. It was sad that his family members saw him in the light that they did. I suddenly could see the pain that he held inside, and part of me wanted to love it away somehow. I wanted to prove his family wrong about Dustin and me. I wanted them to see that he did deserve me, and that we were going to be happy whether they liked it or not.

Eventually, he took me to meet his grandmother. She was a sweet and an unassuming woman. She had a round plump face, and a very tender voice. I loved everything about her. He told me that he considered her to be more of his mother than his natural mother was.

One day she told him how beautiful that she thought I was. To this, Dustin said, "She is? I had not noticed." His words stung. If he did not find me beautiful at all, then why was he dating me? Why was he wanting to get serious with me?

My thoughts were quickly interrupted. "Angelica," Dustin said excitedly. "Look at my grandmother's ring." I glanced over at his grandmother's wrinkled hand. On her finger was a beautiful ring that had scroll carvings in the sides and a pink heart-shaped ruby in the center.

"That ring was purchased by my father when he was serving in our military across the sea. He gave it as a gift to my grandmother. It has been passed through the family, and someday it will come to me." I thought that was a wonderful gift for his father to have given her, and I thought that he must be a gentle man under his rough exterior.

"It is a very beautiful ring." I said. "It really does look like it is a very unique shade of pink.", "It is." Dustin stated. "It is rare for a ruby to be that pink."

It was not long before Dustin took me back to the spot under the tree where we first met and asked me to marry him. Inside, I was screaming "No!" But I said yes instead. I did not feel like I expected to feel once I was engaged to be married.

I felt emotionless, empty, and part of me questioned why I would go through with such a crazy idea. I wondered, "Do I really expect something built on such a faulty foundation to last a long time?" I knew that he was not the man that I was looking for, I continued to choose to believe that I had lost that man forever.

I also believed that he would not accept me now that I had been through all that I had. This really was the only opportunity for marriage that I would ever have. I truly believed that. And what a sad thing it was that I did.

On a cold, dreary and very rainy day during the summer after I turned 19, we were married. There was nothing really spectacular about that day. In fact, it was a miserable day, and not only because of the weather.

I turned to leave the wedding alter, and the man who just married us pulled me to the side. "Angelica," He warned. "This marriage is going to be hard." He handed me the tokens of our wedding vows, then continued. "I am giving these to you because you will need to remind Dustin that you are his wife and that you have certain rights as his wife."

He said that I would need to remind him who owned him. This disturbed me greatly. "Who can own someone?" I thought. "Why would he say something like that?"

Shortly after that, Dustin changed. It was like he was an entirely different person. While I was happy to receive congratulations and gifts from friends and family, he wanted to leave. He wanted nothing to do with any of the wedding celebrations. He wanted to just go home and go to bed.

This saddened me a great deal. I hoped that my wedding day would be a good one. That we would both be happy, and that Dustin would be glad that he married me. That definitely was not the experience that I was having.

We went to Dustin's parents' large and spacious hut for a quick meal. While there, his mother continually mocked our wedding day. "Oh look at your wonderful wedding day!" she laughed as she pointed out how much it was raining outside.

She floated off to the kitchen to finish some last minute preparations for some of the food. We began to open the gifts that had been given to us. Many family members were still present and were making comments about each of the gifts. All of them were very positive, which helped to lighten my mood.

I unwrapped a beautiful work of art. I was so happy with it that I exclaimed, "Look Dustin! Isn't this gorgeous?!" As Dustin turned my way, his mother came into the room and said, "Where ever would you put that?! The hut that Dustin has gotten for the two of you is far too small. You would have to hang it on the ceiling." I went silent.

I held back feelings of anger, tears and remorse as I looked at the giver of the gift, my grandmother, and said, "Thank you so much for the art. I really love it."

At that moment, I had enough. I wanted to leave. We had plans to honeymoon at a little inn that was away from the village. I was looking forward to enjoying that beautiful destination and getting away from Dustin's mother. "Dustin," I whispered, "We better go so that we can get to our destination on time." Dustin gathered up his things from the wedding ceremony, and we left for the hut that he had found for us.

When I walked in the door of my new home, I noticed that it was very small, but I did not care. I liked that it was simple and organized. There was room for all of the essential things. I knew that we were just starting out and I did not expect to have everything.

I asked Dustin, "Where is your bag?" "What bag?" He replied. "The one you packed for our honeymoon." I said. Dustin looked at me for a moment, then said, "I have not packed it yet." I was shocked. We had been planning this day for months, and we had discussed packing the night before the wedding for our honeymoon so that we could just leave quickly.

I was furious, but I didn't want to let him know it. Feelings of not being important and feelings of rejection started to fill my soul. I didn't say anything. I just fumed inside and waited.

Dustin grabbed some of his clothing that had been stuffed haphazardly in the corner and shoved them into a bag. There didn't seem to be any thought put into what he was bringing. Then he said, "Now that I'm packed, let's rest for a while." I said, "OK."

I was very confused. I thought that we were leaving. I did not want to cause any conflict, so I just laid down. As we drifted off to sleep, I worried about the plans that we had made, and if the timing of them would still work out whenever it was that we actually left.

After a short time of resting, Dustin rolled over and started kissing me. I thought that he wanted to consummate our marriage. "Do you want to make love here or when we get to our honeymoon destination?" I inquired. He replied, "I do not plan on having sex anytime soon. Sex means that there will be children, and I do not want to have any for a while."

I was stunned. Long before we married we talked about children. We discussed how we wanted to have them right away. I did not understand this sudden change. Not only that, but I thought, "Who gets married and then doesn't want to have sex?!" I felt deep down that something must be wrong.

Dustin sensed that I was not happy about the situation, and he started kissing me again. He started to unbutton my dress, and then take his clothes off. After sex ended, he said, "I really didn't enjoy that. It felt gross."

I was deeply hurt. I had hoped that after everything I had been through to have a good experience with sex, especially with the man that I had married. It was then that I realized that I had made another mistake, but I had too much pride to admit it to anyone.

I was determined to make it work no matter what. I was not going to be one of those women who ended up divorced. I was not going to be like my mother. My marriage was going to make it through anything.

I truly believed that no matter what happened, that it could all work out for our good. That we would be a stronger couple that we would be able to work through these issues. Dustin hopped up and said "Let's go." And with that, we headed off to our honeymoon destination.

Chapter 7

Increasing Loneliness

I've been a married woman now for two weeks. I feel like I am alone in the world. I have not seen my family for a long time, and Dustin has been working a lot. I never would have thought that it was possible to share a life with someone and feel so alone. I sense more now than ever that something is wrong.

Dustin does not act like he is close to me at all. He is very distant. I have heard of old couples growing apart, but how can people who have been married for two weeks already have separated into such separate worlds?

Comfort whispers, "Angelica, something is very wrong. You need to prepare yourself." I was suddenly filled with fear. I was not sure that I wanted to know what was wrong. I felt that I have had enough pain in my life. I did not want anymore. I felt angry.

That night, when Dustin came in late, he sat on the edge of our bed. "Angelica," he began. "I need to tell you something." My breath caught in my throat as I braced myself for whatever was coming.

He continued, "I have not been faithful to our wedding vows. I have been spying on the women who have been bathing in the lake whenever I go to work. I can't help it. I have secretly been spying on them for years. I thought by getting married that I could stop, but I can't. I have been feeling so guilty. I'm sorry."

My eyes immediately filled with tears that continually burst forth like a never ending fountain. I felt like the tears were never going to stop. "How could he do this to me?!" I thought. "How could he hurt me this way knowing all that I have been through?"

My mind raced through all of the different reasons why I married this man. Characteristics and situations that I thought would guarantee his love for me, keep me safe, and ensure that I would not ever be betrayed. I became angry with myself for being so naïve, so trusting, and for thinking that I could possibly choose someone that would not hurt me.

It was in that moment that I realized that Dustin did not love me. He loved his habit of looking at the village women naked more than he loved me. He made it clear that he felt guilty, but he did not stop himself from doing it. He had lied to me. He had deceived me about who he was. I felt devastated and humiliated.

I did not want my mother or anyone to know that Dustin had broken our vows. That he had lusted after other women. Several of them.

Within a few weeks, I started to compare myself to them. I wondered who they were, and why they were able to get my husband's attention more than I was. I started to look for what was wrong with me. Why I did not measure up, and what it was that needed to be different.

I felt very confused. Just a few months ago I had several young men interested in me. I could have chosen anyone of them. Instead, I chose Dustin, who I was not even attracted to. I pondered about how I was being rejected by someone like him. I started to question if I was good enough for anyone at all. If I was attractive enough, sexy enough.

One night before he went to work, I approached him about it. I said quietly, "Dustin, I want to be everything to you." he replied, "Angelica, you will never be everything to me." I fell silent.

His words cut me like a knife deep into my heart. I focused all the energy I could to stop the pain from boiling to the surface. I tried to numb myself to the pain, bury it down deep, and force myself to feel nothing at all in order to remain calm and collected on the outside. And it was then that I came to the conclusion that I would never be good enough.

Each day Dustin came home late I knew that he had been watching the women in our town bathe. I questioned what I should do. I did not want the women to be watched without their knowledge, and I did not want to lose my husband to a fantasy that was only in his mind. I was filled with rage. I wanted to destroy the lake where the women bathed.

Some days when I was hurting deeply, I would long for the women to go away. To never bathe there again. To keep their clothes on. I started to blame them for my husband's actions. It seemed easier to do than to confront my true feelings about him and myself.

When the pain had reached a higher level than I thought I could bare, I determined that I would talk to my mother-in-law about it. "Mom," I confided, "I don't know why, but Dustin has told me that he has been sneaking around to look at the women naked while they are bathing." She replied, "Perhaps if you gave him enough sex and took better care of yourself dear he wouldn't have a reason to do that."

I was shocked. I thought, "How could a mother not care about the harm that her son was doing to himself, or to his wife?" I was very confused. My husband was demanding sex from me every day, sometimes several times a day. I thought that his parents had the same beliefs about the importance of marriage vows and keeping them. With this revelation, I felt even more alone than I did before.

I told myself that there was no one to turn to, no one to talk to about this secret that was causing me so much pain. It was in that moment that I decided to keep Dustin's secret to myself from that point forward.

I turned my focus to having children of my own. Perhaps, I could find some goodness in all of the pain I was feeling. I had committed to being married to this man, so I might as well make the most of it.

It was not long before I discovered that I was pregnant. I felt excited, only to miscarry after a few weeks. I started to wonder if I would ever feel happy again. If I would ever stop feeling lonely. I wanted to make friends, but Dustin told me to stay in the hut whenever he was gone.

I had not gotten the chance to get to know very many people. Sherry and I grew apart, and eventually we never spoke to each other anymore. I no longer had dinner with everyone in town. Dustin wanted me to eat at home alone.

I had no idea the kind of danger I was in, or how small my world was getting. I was trying to only survive it. As time went on, Dustin moved us to another hut, and then another hut. Each hut was farther and farther away from family and everyone I knew.

I saw Dustin less and less. When I did see him, he would say something critical to me. He would tell me that he did not like what I was wearing, how my hair was done, or even say he didn't want to kiss me or hold me.

One time when he came home, I was excited to see him. I ran up to him to kiss him, and he grabbed me by each arm and threw me to the floor. The feeling of rejection was far more painful than the physical impact of hitting the floor. I wrote my mother about what happened, and continued to try to build my marriage in these circumstances.

Suddenly one day, I felt really sick. "Dustin," I said, "I feel horrible. I feel like I am going to throw up!" And within seconds, I was heaving so hard that it felt like my insides were going to come up too. Dustin looked at me and said, "I bet that you are pregnant." I thought that it wasn't possible to be pregnant again so soon.

"Maybe I have caught something." I replied. "No," he said, "I think that you are definitely with child." "I guess we will know in time." I said. And with that, he went out the door to go to work. My mind started racing through the events of the last few weeks trying to determine if it was even possible for me to be pregnant.

My heart started to overflow with emotions. There was a sense of joy at the possibility of having a child, of not being alone. However, there was also the fear that this baby would die too. I was not sure that I could bare it.

As the weeks passed, it became very clear to me that I was indeed pregnant. Dustin seemed to become a little bit kinder to me. One night, he invited me to come with him to work. While he was working, I wandered outside. I walked through the tall grass, and I enjoyed the moonlight shining down on me.

Down below, I saw a lake. Even though I realized that this lake was the place where I was being betrayed each and every night over and over again, I could not help but be drawn to it.

As I reached the water's edge, I felt a sudden urge to swim. I took off everything except for my under clothes, and jumped into the water. It was warm and inviting. I did not care if anyone saw me.

I swam around until I was nearly exhausted. I climbed out of the water, and was determined to do a backflip back into the lake like I did when I was younger. As I came to the surface, I knew that doing a backflip had been a mistake. I felt very sick.

I questioned if I would be able to make it back to where Dustin was. I struggled to get my clothes back on, and I wandered inside. As soon as he saw me, Dustin's face went pale. "What have you been doing?" he asked.

"I went for a swim." I said. "You don't look good at all. Are you ok?" he questioned. "I am going to be sick." I whispered, as I ran over to a bush and threw up. I felt exhausted. I curled up in a ball on the floor, and waited until it was time to go home. Eventually, I fell asleep.

I woke up to the sound of birds singing. I was covered in furs, and I felt much better. "Here," Dustin said, as he handed me a piece of ginger root. "I think it will help." I nibbled at the ginger root slowly. I did not want to throw up again. My stomach did not do any flip flops, and I realized that I was going to be ok. It was then that I realized I was home, and I had no idea how I had gotten there.

"How did I get here?" I asked. Dustin replied, "We walked here. You were pretty much asleep the entire way." "Oh," I said surprised. I slowly got up and started to make some breakfast. I immediately felt like I had to sit down because I felt light headed again.

"Don't worry about that." He said. Then Dustin grabbed a chair and had me sit down. "I will take care of everything." He said as he started the fire and grabbed a pan and some eggs.

Dustin had never done anything like this for me before. I wondered why he was doing it. I figured that it must be for the child that was in my womb, because he did not do things like this for me ever.

Months went by. I was constantly sick. My throwing up became so intense that I was afraid to eat anything at all. It reached a point where the heaving was so hard, that it burst vessels in my throat and I would throw up blood with anything I ate.

I could not wait until the nausea came to an end. It felt like I had given up everything good in my life in exchange for never ending exhaustion and vomiting.

After some time, I felt well again. I started going out more and enjoying nature. The first time that I felt the baby move, I sensed its personality. He was joyful and I felt that he had a sense of humor as he bounced from side to side. I felt a little motion sickness sometimes from the amount of flips he would do at a time. However, feeling this life growing inside me made me feel very happy.

One day, I was walking along the top of a hill when some man came running out of nowhere. He hit me hard, knocking me down the hill. I was disoriented and not sure what had really happened. Everything went black.

When I came to, I started to climb the hill. A woman came rushing down and hit into me again. I grabbed my stomach and collapsed to the ground. I wanted my mother. I knew something was wrong.

When Dustin arrived home and did not find me there, he went searching for me. He found me near the hill, and he helped me get home. He laid me in bed, and got me some water. I could feel that I was bleeding. I couldn't feel the baby moving anymore. I was afraid to say anything to anyone.

"Dustin" I said in a choked up voice, "I needed my mother." He sent for her. It had been so long since we had seen each other. She decided that she would bring my brothers and sisters with her, and they would live in our village now, so that she could take care of me.

"Mom," I whispered when I saw her. "I can't feel the baby move anymore. I am concerned. I think that he is dead." My mother tried to reassure me. "Angelica, you took a nasty fall. Maybe the baby is just being quiet."

I started contracting, and so my mother determined to give me some herbs that prevent miscarriage. The cramping and bleeding stopped. I assumed that I should not worry about not feeling the baby move anymore. I was inexperienced. I had never had a baby before. I told myself I was just being paranoid.

Two weeks went by, and my stomach did not seem to be growing any bigger. I still had not felt the baby move. Dustin decided that it was time that I saw a doctor.

As the doctor finished his examination, I whispered to Dustin, "I think that the baby is dead." Dustin responded, "No, the baby is fine. Stop worrying." The feeling in my gut that the baby had died only intensified. I knew that he was dead. I knew that he was not there anymore. I no longer felt his presence in me. I wanted to be wrong, but I knew that I wasn't.

The doctor and his assistant stepped outside to discuss what they had found in hushed voices. I knew what was coming. "Dustin," the doctor said as he returned. "I am sorry to tell you this, but your baby is dead. There are no signs that it is alive. We believe that it would be best to make your wife go into labor so that she doesn't die from an infection."

Dustin looked at me in shock. He fell to his knees, and he started sobbing. He screamed out "No! No!" as he tried to wipe tears from his face. I stood there silently. I did not know what to do. I knew that with how far along I was that I would have to go through labor. I knew that my pain, my battle had just begun.

I reached over and cradled Dustin in my arms. In that moment, I cared more about whether or not he was ok than I did about myself. I held him while he cried for several minutes. I became the rock he needed. No one seemed to think about the fact that I needed someone to cry to, someone to lean on. Once again, I felt that I had no choice than to be the strong one and stand alone on my own.

"We suggest that your wife go into labor right away." The doctor said urgently. Dustin replied, "How do I know you are right? What if the baby is not dead? I do not want to be responsible for killing my own child!"

The doctor stated coolly, "We know for certain that your baby has died. There has been no more growth and your wife has not felt the child move. You really should not wait to do this, but we will give you some time." With that, the doctor picked up his bag and he and his assistant walked out the door.

I turned to my mother. "I'm so sorry, Angelica." She said, with tears glistening in her eyes. I glanced at Dustin still sitting on the floor. "Dustin," I said gently. "I think that the doctor is right. I think that I have to do this."

My mother immediately ran after the doctor and told him that we were going to do it. "My assistant and I will be over later tonight." He told her.

I tried to prepare myself to deliver my dead child. I had no idea how I was going to do that. I had never seen anyone give birth. I understood the basics of it, but I was not sure how much the pain would be.

Darkness began to set in as the doctor's assistant arrived. She told me that the doctor would be arriving soon, and that she would get things going. She was very kind and gentle. She kept reassuring me that everything was going to be ok. She addressed each of the concerns that I had.

She told me that she came at the time that she did to try to give me as much privacy as possible. She did not want me to feel like everyone in the village was going to be aware of what was going on and gather outside. I appreciated her doing this for me.

Part of me wanted to be alone. Another part of me wanted to just be with my mother. I believed that I was supposed to be strong through this, which is what women do, so I never let anyone know what I was really feeling. I just acted tough.

The truth is that I was devastated. "Is this happening to me because I would be a bad mother? Did I do something wrong? Is this because I married Dustin instead of continuing to travel the path I was on?" I questioned. "I should have stayed inside that day over two weeks ago." I told myself.

I was subconsciously repeating what Dustin had said to me the weeks before. He told me that it was my fault that our son died, because I did not stay in the hut like he had asked me to. I often thought that maybe he was right. The death of our child was my fault because I was in the wrong place at the wrong time.

Just then, there was a knock at the door. Another assistant came in, "Dr. Jones has sent me to take care of Angelica. There is no need for you to stay any longer." she said plainly while staring that the other assistant. The first assistant excused herself, and headed out the door. I immediately felt uncomfortable. I knew that I was not going to like the new assistant. She was cold and uncaring. I was certain that she did not want to be there at all.

The assistant began to give me a whole slew of herbs and had me drink plenty of fluids. Labor began to intensify. As it became more painful, I bent my knees trying to prepare for the baby to be delivered and lessen the pain. The assistant kept trying to force my legs shut. "You need to wait until the doctor arrives." She scolded.

I thought that she was making an impossible request. The herbs that she had given me forced labor to begin. There was nothing I could do to stop it. As the pain increased, I became more and more uncomfortable. A feeling of panic started to overcome me as I worried that the doctor would not get there in time.

Dustin tried to comfort me, but his touch only brought me more pain. I did not want anyone to touch me, especially not him. The assistant kept running in and out of our hut. It was as if she was trying to avoid the situation completely.

I knew that she did not want to deliver my deceased son. She wanted the doctor to be there. Suddenly, my water broke. I told my mom that it had. The assistant was still outside somewhere waiting for the doctor to arrive. The feeling of panic increased, and I felt the baby's body moving down into position. Just then I heard screaming outside. This put me in a panic.

My mother came over and saw that the baby was starting to come out breech. She knew that I needed help, and since the assistant was nowhere to be found, my mother started to deliver the baby. She was able to deliver all of him except his head, and that is when the assistant returned.

I was already furious with the assistant. I could not believe that she left me and my mother to deal with this on our own. When she came between my legs to finish delivering the baby, I had an overwhelming urge to just grab her hair and pull it has hard as I could. I didn't do it, but it would not have taken much effort to get a good grip on her cotton like hair.

"Push" the assistant firmly said. "I am!" I screamed at her. Just then the baby's head came out. The assistant lifted the baby up. I could see that it was a boy. A boy that looked just like Dustin.

A very miniature version of Dustin laid in her hands. I was startled that he looked so much like a little adult. For a split second, it seemed as if I was looking at my husband lying there dead. It was very disturbing.

The assistant rushed off to the side with my son to clean him off. Just then the doctor arrived. He started talking to everyone else in the room. It felt as if I was not even there.

I felt another contraction and pushed out the afterbirth. Just then the doctor said, "We just have to wait until she is ready to deliver the afterbirth." "I already have." I stated calmly.

The doctor walked over to the bed lifted the sheet, and said "It's true." He picked up the placenta and began to tell everyone how it worked, and show where the baby had come out of it.

The doctor gave me something to help me sleep, and then his assistant brought my son over by me. She asked me if I wanted to hold him. I shook my head.

I had never held a dead body, and I was afraid to do it. Part of me really wanted to hold him, but I did not know if it was really ok to do it. There really was no one to guide me through this experience. Even though there were people there, I felt really isolated.

Eventually everyone left except for Dustin, and the medication the doctor gave me took effect. I was able to fall into a deep sleep. While I was sleeping, I could somehow see Dustin sitting in the chair at the foot of the bed watching me.

The assistant showed up in the middle of the night to check on me. When she did so, she laughed about how out of it I was. She kept lifting my arm and dropping it. Each time she let go of it and let it free fall to the bed, it would hit the edge of the bedframe hard. It hurt, and I found myself feeling very angry that Dustin did not stop her.

When I woke up in the morning, I asked Dustin why he did not stop her. "How could you have seen that?!" he questioned. "You were completely asleep." "I don't know" I said. It was obvious that I had seen it. It made me wonder if the medication somehow had made my spirit leave my body for a time. I felt uneasy.

After resting a few more hours, I got up and looked in the mirror. I was shocked at how angelic I looked. I wondered how I could look like that with all that I just went through. I thought to myself that we really cannot know what someone has gone through just by looking at them.

My heart was broken, I was devastated, but anyone looking at me would not have been able to see that. They would just see my innocent hazel eyes, and my long brown hair with blond highlights glistening in the light. I determined in that moment to never judge someone by how they appear on the outside, to take the time to find out how they really feel on the inside.

A few days later I became very ill. I had a high fever, and I began to hallucinate. "Bring me some blankets." I begged. I believed that I was laying outside naked in the snow. I kept asking for blankets because I felt so cold. My mother realized that not all the afterbirth had gotten out of my body, so she gave me some herbs to help.

Dustin came with me to the lake to help me bathe. It was hard for me to stand in the water because I was so weak. I appreciated him being willing to come with me, but I was scared. I tried to share how I felt with him. "Dustin, I feel so sick. I have never been this sick in my life. I am afraid that I might die." He continued to wash me off as if I hadn't said anything, and then eventually responded, "If it is your time, it is your time."

He was so uncaring and emotionless when he said it, that it cut me to the center. I felt that he did not really love me once again, and he did not care if I lived or not. My salty tears ran down my cheeks like a waterfall into the lake below.

Later that night, Dustin wanted to have sex. I had a bad feeling about it, but in that moment, I believed that I should not deny my husband sex when he wanted it.

Comfort whispered, "Don't do it. Do not let him have sex with you. He will violate you." My inner voice said, "Angelica, this is not right. The timing is not right and you just had a baby." I ignored both voices. As soon as he started having sex with me, I started to see images in my mind.

I saw a woman from the village. She was very skinny, almost boney. She was so thin that she looked more like a child than a woman. Her hair was short and a dirty blonde color. I had a strong impression come over me, that she was in Dustin's mind. I saw her face become a mask over my face, and I could bear no more. "Are you thinking about a woman from the village with short blond hair instead of me right now?" I asked Dustin.

"Yes," he said surprised. "I was pretending that I was with her just now." My heart was broken into even smaller pieces. I cried. I shoved him off of me, "I hate you! I hate that you ever made me care about you!"

How cruel he was. What man would think about another woman while using the body of his wife? Who would do that to someone who was mourning the death of their son? It took everything in me to not tackle him to the ground and start punching him in the face. It took an incredible amount of self-control to pull myself together. I sat up pulling my knees into my chest while wrapping my arms around them.

Dustin got up, walked to the door and stepped out into the darkness. He went to go see his parents. I turned to my mother for comfort. Hours later he returned. He told me that he did not like what he had learned about his father while he was gone.

He said he had told his father all that had happened, and his father said that he would have been unfaithful to his mother, but no one was willing. He determined that he did not want to be a man like that, so he came back to me to apologize.

A few months went by, and I started feeling sick again. I knew I was pregnant, and I knew that there was more than one baby. Dustin and the doctor thought I just wanted to be pregnant, and that there was no way that I could possibly know I was carrying twins.

I continued to tell them that I knew that one was a boy and one was a girl, and that the girl would be born first. They seemed to think that I had just gone a little crazy and it was just wishful thinking.

It was not long before it became obvious that I was pregnant, and that there was more than one baby inside of me. My mother was the first person, besides myself, that was able to feel both of the babies move. She never doubted me. She knew that I knew my own body, and so I was very happy that she got to have that experience.

It was at this time, that there was some commotion in the village, and word came that someone new was moving in. I went to the window to see who the new neighbors were and was shocked when I saw Anthony. Not only was he in the village, he was coming to my door! "Dustin! I do not want to see him!" I screamed. I wanted to pretend that I was not home, but Dustin was having none of it. He walked straight to the door of the hut and opened it. "Hi." He said as he motioned for Anthony to come in.

Once Anthony came in the door, he started talking with Dustin. They laughed for a while and then Anthony suddenly stated that he had come to apologize to me. "Why don't you and Angelica talk outside for a while," Dustin suggested.

I reluctantly stood up and walked out the door. Anthony and I sat by each other just outside on the porch. "Angelica," Anthony said, "I have made a lot of changes in my life, and because of that I need to tell you the truth about something." By now I had learned that when a man comes to me and says something like that, it is never a good thing.

I was still recovering from the shock of these two men getting along with each other. I definitely did not see Anthony's confession coming. "Angelica, it was me that set up the log trap that knocked you unconscious. At the time, I was hoping that it would kill you."

"What?!" I exclaimed totally shocked and terrified at the same time. He continued, "If I could not have you as my wife, then I thought that no one should. When I saw that it did not kill you, I saw an opportunity and took advantage of it." I stared at the ground blankly. "I thought that by having sex with you that it would convince you to stay with me."

As he continued to confess to me, I admired his honesty, but at the same time, I wanted to hit him as hard as I could over and over again. What he did to me completely changed the way that I looked at myself and my life. I had made different choices than I would have had I felt better about myself.

Because of what I believed about myself, and how I interpreted that experience, I had married someone that I really did not love. Someone that I was not really attracted to. Someone who I thought was the only person on earth that would accept my past and me.

"I forgive you." I said, and went back into the hut. Dustin passed me on his way to the door. He stepped outside and continued to talk to Anthony. They continued to talk about me. Over the next several weeks, they continued to spend time together.

I would often walk into the hut and hear them talking about my body, what they both liked about it, and what great legs I had. It felt horribly wrong to have the man who raped me talking to my husband and both of them discussing my body like I am just an object for their sexual pleasure.

One morning I determined that I had enough of it, "Dustin, I do not want to ever see Anthony over here again! I cannot believe that you would want to spend one moment with the man that raped me!" It was the first time that I spoke out in anger, and surprisingly, Dustin listened. He said that he understood why I would not like it, and that he would not spend time with him anymore.

Chapter 8

Distorted Perceptions

My body was changing rapidly. It was hard to do the simplest tasks. I was tired all the time, and I struggled to do my daily chores. Eventually the doctor stated that I needed to be on bed rest in order to ensure the safety and health of the babies.

Dustin often came home angry. He complained that I was always in bed. "Of course I am." I would state firmly. "I am doing what the doctor told me was best for my babies."

My first son's death had made me much more cautious and careful. I was very protective of the babies because I realized just how fragile life really is.

"Angelica, it feels really awkward to be around you or to be intimate with you. It feels like there is someone in the middle of everything." It hurt that Dustin was not attracted to me anymore. That he was constantly pointing out what was wrong with my body and how I looked, dressed or acted.

I knew that I was doing the best I could for the babies, and that is what I focused on. I lost a lot of weight at first due to the morning sickness, but eventually I got it under control. Once that struggle ended, a new one began.

My body had a hard time growing at the rate that the babies did. My stomach began to itch and burn. Eventually, my skin stretched so far apart that giant red marks appeared on my belly.

I worried that I scratched myself too hard and made myself bleed. I went to my mother worried and concerned. "Mom," I said, "I think that I scratched myself so hard that I am bleeding."

She took a look at my stomach and declared, "Those are stretch marks, and they are a normal part of being pregnant." Then she took a moment to show me the stretch marks that she had from being pregnant. It brought me a lot of comfort, and I stopped worrying about it and focused on how to find relief from the itching.

Dustin continued to watch the women bathe whenever he was stressed, wanted to escape life, or was bored. Every time I became aware of what he was doing, I would cry alone in the dark corners and spaces of our hut.

I would often look at my reflection and wish that I was good enough to keep my own husband's interest. I longed for true affection, fidelity and trust. I often told myself that this is a choice that I made, and that I have to live with it. I looked forward to when the twins would be born. I focused on being a mother, and how I would raise them.

The day soon arrived when I knew that the twins were going to be born. I told the doctor that I knew that labor was starting. He sent his assistant to my hut to check on me.

"Angelica, it's too soon for these babies to come. Your body is not ready. You should just rest." I was adamant that she get the doctor. I told her, "This is unacceptable! I demand to see the doctor now! I will only rest if he tells me that I really am not going to have these babies today!"

His assistant was startled, she literally shook as she scurried out the door to get him. The doctor arrived quickly. He examined me and declared "This little mama is right, these babies are on their way out right now."

As labor progressed, the doctor discovered that the twins were both breech. There was no way to safely get them out, so he determined that a C-section was necessary.

Dustin was horrified at the idea. He himself had been born by C-section, and he did not want to have his children or wife go through the same experience that his own mother had. He became very ill after he was born and he feared that the same was going to happen to his children.

The doctor hung up a large blue cloth in front of my face, then he prepared to make the incision. I had been given herbs for pain, but there was no way to completely eliminate it.

As I was being cut open, I said "I can feel that!" The doctor asked me if it hurt horribly, and I said it was burning and stinging. He said that the herbs are working fine. If they weren't, it would have felt a lot worse than that.

At that moment, I looked up at Dustin's face. All the blood had rapidly drained out of it. He was a ghostly pale white. Seeing him like this caused me to panic, and I began to go into shock.

The doctor's assistant stuck her face right in mine. "Angelica, pay attention to me. Listen to my voice. You are ok. Your babies are almost here." She spoke in such a soothing tone that I began to calm down. I felt a huge release of pressure as the first baby was pulled out of my stomach. The doctor exclaimed, "It's a beautiful little girl!"

Two minutes later, a little boy joined her. When I was finally able to see them, they were as different as could be. The little girl had brown hair and brown eyes, and the little boy was blond with blue eyes. I determined to name them right then. I named the girl Aurora and the boy August.

August was slightly bigger than Aurora. He wanted to stay by his sister, he kept trying to move closer to her, but she wanted her space. She had been crammed into a little ball the entire time that she was in my womb.

"Angelica," the doctor said gently, "Your babies are going to need additional care for a while. They have arrived early and they need to be watched closely. My assistant and I will take turns being here with you for the next several days."

It was hard to watch the babies struggle, but I was grateful for them. My dead son was not far from my thoughts. Once I had recovered, I began to care for the babies with my mother's and Dustin's help. Eventually, I established a routine, and life went back to normal. As normal as it could anyway.

One day while I was changing my clothes, Dustin came into the room and stared at my stomach. He came up to me and ran his fingers across it gently. "You look like you are starving." He said. "I cannot believe that you are this small. Your skin looks like you got a really bad and painful burn. You look nothing like you used to." He stated flatly. I felt horrible. I suddenly missed my old body, and was ashamed at the changes that I had experienced. I started to hate myself even more.

Several weeks later, Dustin came home from work with fabric that he had found at work. He asked me to take my clothes off. I thought he was going to see if it was a good color for a new dress or something, but instead, he used it to bind my stomach and attempted to hide it from his view. He smiled as he saw that his idea was a success.

"Now you look hot." He said. I realized that he was hiding my stomach in order to make my body look like it used to. I felt even worse about myself. I felt used and that there was only one thing that he valued about me.

I began to lose weight. I became smaller than I was before I had the twins. Dustin started to complain that I was too thin. He stated multiple times that he wished that I was full-figured like his grandmother. It was then that I realized that no matter what I did, that it was not ever going to be enough for him.

I would never be just fine the way that I am. I started to get angry. I had sacrificed my body to have these children, and here he was putting me down every few days. I refused to let anyone know that I was angry, and I stuffed any negative feelings anytime they came up.

One day I decided that I was going to clean and reorganize the hut. I came across an old box that Dustin had when he used to travel. His parents had brought it over, and I had not taken the time to look at it.

As soon as I opened it, I had an uncomfortable feeling come over me. I sensed that this box contained dark secrets. I was afraid to touch anything. Being as curious as I am, I could not stay away from it either.

As I looked through the box, I came across several pictures of Dustin's sister. As soon as I touched one of them, images flashed through my mind. They were horrible images. I felt sick to my stomach. I was terrified that they may be real, that they were images of true events. I felt the need to find out what the truth was.

The next moment that I saw Dustin, I confronted him. I asked him "When you were traveling, did you take pictures of your sister with you so you could focus on sexual thoughts and feelings about her?" He looked at me in total shock and collapsed in a heap on the floor crying. With his eyes wide with bewilderment he asked, "How did you know?!" I explained to him that I saw it in my mind when I touched the pictures of his sister he had. He kept crying. I had no idea what I should do.

Suddenly, Aurora started to cry. Dustin said he would take care of her. I sat on the edge of our bed, and felt feelings of shock and horror take over me. Just then I heard a piercing scream from Aurora.

I ran back to her room and asked "What is going on?!" He said "I don't know." I glanced around the room quickly, looking for clues. I saw that he had been changing her diaper, and that he had left red handprints on her thighs from forcing her legs apart so far. I was terrified what that meant.

I started asking him what he did to her, why the handprints were on her thighs, and if he was doing something that he should not have. He got mad and started screaming hysterically at me, "I love my sister. I wish I would have married her instead of you!"

I was shocked and hurt. He ran away from me to the main living area, and kept screaming. "I used to spy on her when she was young! I watched her and her friends as they were changing clothing when they went swimming together! It was a long time ago!" He continued to stomp around the room. August woke up and began to fuss. I grabbed him, and brought him into the room with Aurora and me.

Suddenly Dustin blurted "I used to sneak into her room and try to see her naked while she was asleep when she was a little girl!" I became completely horrified and nauseous. I immediately realized that his sister would have only been 3 years old when he started to do the things that he was talking about. I could not help but relive all of my own feelings of how I felt when I was being molested around that same age.

"Dustin," I said incredulously. "Have you done things like this to our children? Have you thought these kinds of thoughts about them?" He replied, "I have been afraid of having those kinds of thoughts and of doing something." "Do you really think you could hurt our children?" I asked.

Just then Dustin started screaming. He grabbed anything that he could get his hands on and started throwing the objects at the wall beside me. I was afraid for my life, and the lives of my children. I grabbed them both and ran off into the night.

I reached a neighboring hut where two single women lived together. One of them sent for my mother, while the other tried to comfort me and the children.

My mother arrived, and she took the kids and me to stay with her. She contacted the village council to discuss what had happened. The head of the council requested that Dustin meet with him, and then he had to meet with the protective council as well.

I stayed with my mother for some time. During the time that I stayed with her, Dustin came to visit. Instead of trying to repair things, he continually degraded me and put me down. He told me that he wished that I had red hair, that I was taller, and that I was like a woman that he worked with.

One day he came over to my mother's hut and said, "I wish you could get pregnant as easy as the woman at work. She never had a baby die." He continued to point out that our son died because of me. I became so angry, that I literally grabbed him and threw him out the door and off the porch. Then slammed the door closed behind him.

I could not see any way that my marriage could be reconciled. I felt that it was too unsafe, but I also had no idea how I could provide for the kids and myself. I worried about feeding them, getting them the things that they needed, and how I would be able to be the mother that they needed. It was about that time that I discovered that I was pregnant again.

I believed that there was no way I could be pregnant and take care of the kids by myself. I knew that I would have to be on bed rest again, so I determined to return to Dustin.

I went into our hut alone having left the twins with my mother. Dustin was lying on our bed. "I need to talk to you." I whispered. He reached up, grabbed me by the back of the neck while pulling me towards him and started to kiss me. Then he pulled me to the bed beside him.

I felt very tense and uncomfortable, and I braced myself for what was coming. Whatever it was, I had convinced myself that it was the price that I was going to have to pay in order to have him provide for the kids and me.

He continued to kiss me and take off my clothes. Once I was completely naked and vulnerable, he began to talk about the woman at work again.

I began to feel my entire being overflow with intense emotional pain, but I held it in and tried to do everything I could to ignore it. I let him do whatever and say whatever he wanted. I did not fight him anymore, I surrendered.

He talked about this other woman while he touched me sexually. He talked about how he wished that he was touching her. Wished that he was with her. I had never been in such total and complete pain inside in my life. Every touch was like a razor blade. I felt myself slowly dying by a thousand cuts.

I was angry with myself for letting him treat me like this. I felt angry at him for doing it. I began to hate all other women that he ever stared at or wanted. I blamed them all for my pain. I held them accountable for his actions because of what they chose to wear and how they acted around him.

Something inside of me was too afraid to hold him accountable and responsible for his own actions. I turned to blaming myself. I believed that it was my fault it happened, that it was all because I was not good enough. I began to despise everything about me.

****

A few months later, a beautiful little girl was placed in my arms. I named her Zinnia. My children were the only source of joy in my life. They were the goodness I could see in the world. There was not much else that brought me joy.

I continued to fight a great deal of feelings of depression, self-hatred and betrayal. I never let anyone know that I was suffering. I just kept living my life day in and day out. I was determined to just keep surviving and being strong.

I became distant and unattached to those around me. I rarely discussed what I felt, what I was going through, and became even more anti-social. My sole purpose was to raise my children.

I decided to ignore a lot of the things that Dustin did and focused on the children. After several months we were like strangers living in the same house. I became pregnant many times after that, and miscarried every time.

Several months passed, and I discovered I was pregnant again. The doctor told me that it was triplets, but only one child survived. I named that sweet looking little boy Zeus.

All my children were very good. They did something that made me laugh every day. They made a lot of messes, but a majority of the time I was entertained by them. They would bring me flowers and talk to me about everything.

As time passed, Dustin and I became more financially successful. He bought us a very large hut, which had additional space that we did not need. In order to make more money, we rented it out to single women. Eventually, we rented it out to my brother Blaze's fiancé so that she could be closer to him.

One afternoon, I walked over to talk with Sadie, my brother's fiancé, and I stumbled upon Dustin staring into her room. I walked up to him quietly and looked in the direction that he was staring. I saw Sadie lying on the floor on her stomach with her skirt hiked up while she was reading. It was obvious that he had been watching her, hoping to get a glimpse of what was under her skirt. I looked at him, gave him a stern look, looked back her direction, and then turned and ran to the cool darkness of our storage area.

Tears were streaming down my face as I knelt in the dark storage room. I could feel the cold, hard concrete through the thin fabric of my skirt as I dug my hand into a nearby wooden shelf and vocally cried out to God.

"Please God. Please save me from the pain! I cannot bear it anymore! This is just too much to ask of me. I cannot live like this. I will do anything for you to take this all away. Please, give him some other problem. Make him eat too much, do drugs or drink. Please anything but this!" I begged. "It is not fair that I have to go through all of this. I am not as strong as you think I am!"

My heart was aching, and there didn't seem to be any way to console myself. My emotional burdens felt as if they were going to completely crush me by their sheer weight. I was shocked at the intensity in which my body continually heaved with each heartfelt sob. I had been through tough things, but nothing that shook me to the core as much as this did. A million questions went through my mind. "Did I make a mistake? Is there something else that I could have done? What could I possibly do?"

I longed for immediate and permanent escape. I wanted to be away from the pain and disappointment. I came to the conclusion that I did not belong in this world. It was too cold and far too harsh for a soul like mine.

Perhaps, I was born at the wrong time, or in the wrong place. Maybe I was meant for better times in a different season of time. I was in the thralls of misery, and it had consumed me. My hopes were thoroughly dashed. I believed that I was trapped, and there was no way out.

Eventually, Dustin lost his job. For nine long months he could not get another one. The tension in the home kept building, and the kids and I did our best to avoid him.

One day, we were not successful in doing that. August was playing with something of mine. I told him to stop and he said "No." Dustin was furious. He came running at our son, grabbed him by his shirt, picked up August and then threw him against the wall. I was terrified. "Stop it!" I screamed.

Dustin pinned August harder against the wall, his shirt gathering tightly around his neck. "Stop! Stop!" I screamed. Dustin became more irate then threw August down the hallway. I heard his body hit the ground with a thud. He started to cry.

Dustin turned towards me and then reached for the door. "How dare you!" I screamed as I started flailing my hands in the air, missing him a majority of the time. "That is not how you treat a child! I am going to go get my mother and the protective council!" With that, I turned to head towards the other door out of the hut.

As I headed toward the door, Dustin became enraged. He grabbed my arm and shouted, "You are not going to tell anyone!" He started to pull on my shirt. I heard the sound of the seams popping and then the ripping of fabric.

The sound of my shirt being destroyed seemed to only inflame his anger. He continued to pull on my shirt, pulling me closer and closer to the floor. I was terrified that if he got me to the floor, that he would beat me to death.

My mind raced throughout the hut thinking about where each of my children were. I did not want anything to happen to them, and I did not want to die.

I grabbed the closest item to where I was, a stone that filled up my entire hand, and hit Dustin in the head with it as hard as I could. It broke in half and cut his head at the same time. Dustin let me go and took off out the door of the hut.

I collapsed to the floor trembling and started to cry. I hurried and got the children. I ran next door, barely able to stand and asked a neighbor to go and get my mother. The protective council came. Eventually they found Dustin, and he confessed to everything. He refused medical treatment saying that he deserved the cut on his head. They brought him back to the hut and sat outside for a while as they prepared to take him away.

Aurora looked outside and saw her father with his hands bound behind his back. She started to scream as they took him away. No matter how hard I tried to comfort her, she continued to scream for hours.

Eventually, a friend from the village showed up to take care of me several hours later. I was still shaking as she tried to comfort me and reassure me that everything was going to be ok. She brought me some fruit to try to help me feel better. Just having someone to talk to helped me a lot.

I realized that I needed to leave that place and go somewhere that would be safer. The kids and I left, and I determined to sell our hut. It sold quickly, and we ended up in a secret community that was for women and children in our situation. Once again, I was faced with how I would survive on my own with four children under the age of three.

One of the conditions that must be met in order to live in this community was to be divorced. I went through the process to legally divorce Dustin. And as promised, a lot of help was offered now that I was a divorcee with children. I was offered a place to live, education, and any other help that I may need. At first it seemed like a dream come true, but then there was Margret.

Margret was the woman who ran the community. Whenever she was around, it felt like I was a prisoner in a jail cell. She demanded perfection in everything within the home. She told me that if she ever saw a crumb on my floor that she was going to kick my kids and me out. The thought of being homeless was terrifying.

Dustin was locked up when he received the divorce papers and signed the papers for the hut to be sold. He had no idea where the kids and I were. He spent 60 days serving his sentence. I was under so much pressure all the time that I started to secretly meet guys in the area just to have someone to talk to.

When Dustin got out, he felt very guilty for all that had happened, and he wanted to change. He started to work on managing his anger, and he waited for the kids and me to contact him.

I really had no plans on ever talking to him again, but one night, I found myself in trouble with a guy that wanted to do more than talk. I got away from him, and the only place I knew to go was my old hut. When I arrived there, Dustin was there too. I talked to him about everything, and we determined that we wanted to work things out.

Both of our families were against us trying to work anything out. They had good reason. We did not want to deal with so many people not wanting us to work things out, so we decided that we would need to move far away. We determined to sell everything we had and move to a village that was far enough away that it would not be easy for them to just show up anytime.

We were remarried in secret. No one learned of our wedding until several days later when we announced we were taking the children and leaving.

Chapter 9

Starting Over

We arrived in our new village under the cover of darkness. It looked empty and much smaller than I had imagined it would. I questioned if I had done the right thing.

I felt an emptiness as I realized that I did not know a single soul besides my husband and children. We had no idea how we were going to make a living or where we were going to live.

We found an inn to stay in for the night. We only had the money that we made selling all that we had. We were not sure that we would be able to find a place to live that we could afford, but we remained hopeful.

In the morning, the owner of the inn came up to us. Puffing on his pipe, he asked "Any chance that you are thinking of living here permanently? Do you need a place to live?" I looked at him surprised, and answered, "Yes, we do."

"All night long I heard the voice of the Creator telling me that you needed a place to stay. And I do have a place for you," the owner of the inn stated.

He led us a short distance to several small huts that were connected together. He showed us a very little one. It only had two rooms. The price was right, so we chose to move into it.

Moving did not take long since we only brought what we could carry with us. We started to settle in, and I hoped that Dustin would find work soon.

A few days later, we met our neighbors George and Pat. They needed help adding a room on to their hut where they were going to move in another area of the village, so Dustin offered to help them. They had land that they did not need, that they offered to sell to us.

We agreed to live there even though it needed a lot of work. We had to deal with a lot of bugs, snakes and other creatures that we did not have to deal with in the mountains.

While the area was lush, green and humid, it did not have the accommodations that the mountain did. The children and I had to haul water from the well a long distance.

We were not used to the hot and humid air, and we struggled a lot with dehydration, and were very uncomfortable. Eventually Dustin got a job at a dairy. He worked long hours, but made good money. We were able to build a better hut, and have the things that we needed.

For six years Dustin worked long hours and I spent my time with the children. I educated them, played with them, and went on many different adventures. As they got older, we decided to move closer to the dairy.

We made new friends and the children and I began to be very involved in the community. We had people over for dinners and discussions. Because Dustin was gone as much as he was, I finally had the freedom to do what I wanted.

When he was home, he was so tired that all he did was sleep. Sometimes he would stay with the children while I went to the market or run other errands.

Life became peaceful, and he never lost his temper again. I started to become well-known in the community. Dustin made a good living. We were able to reach out and help others.

Everyone appreciated my singing and I got to spend a lot of time meeting people and learning new ideas. I started making my own money by watching the young children of single parents in our village.

I had just returned from a successful night of events, when I was startled from my thoughts by the sound of the front door opening and closing. Filling with panic and fear I focused on the fact that Dustin was not supposed to be home for another seven hours.

My heart started pounding so hard in my chest that I worried that it might break through my ribcage and escape into the night. "Dear God," I prayed in my heart silently. "Please help me. Help me be able to handle whatever it is that I am going to face out there."

I slowly reached for an unlit silver candlestick near my writing desk and headed out into the thick darkness of the hall. I raised the candlestick above my head just in case I had to defend myself once more.

I was startled, and my heart skipped a beat the moment that I noticed the silhouette of a man illuminated by the cascading moonlight pouring through the window, slicing through the darkness.

"Angelica," he whispered. "What are you doing here?" I questioned. Dustin slowly lit a candle in the center of the table with a match, then shook his hand to extinguish the little flame once he no longer had any use for it.

"I was fired." he mumbled almost inaudibly. "What?!" I exclaimed. "How is that even possible? You have been working for them for five years! They can't let you go."

Dustin turned towards me slowly and extended his hand. Clasped in his palm I could clearly see the token of our marriage vows. "Give this to the Head Council" he said in a monotone voice. "Why would I need to do that?" I questioned.

A sense of absolute resolve began to envelope me. I immediately felt cold and distant as I drew myself inward for protection. My hair began to stand up on the back of my neck, and a thick tension started to suffocate all the air in the room. I instinctively knew something bad was coming.

"They fired me because they caught me watching the little girls bathe in the lake." Dustin confessed, his eyes turned downwards towards the floor. In total and complete shock, I began to shake my head in disbelief. I could not believe my ears nor my eyes.

Instantly I began to think about all of my broken trust, the years of betrayal, and the lies that had to be lived for the last four years. The moment quickly passed, and I suddenly grew a backbone of ice cold steel. I glared intently as I faced Dustin and stood totally erect. I looked him straight in the eyes with a dagger like stare, and said in a very low and firm tone, "Give it to him yourself!"

I raised my right hand with my arm fully extended and my palm firmly facing Dustin, "I'm done!" I blurted. I whirled around and calmly walked back down the hall. I grabbed my bags and began to pack. A sense of empowerment and freedom filled my being as I recognized that the last fourteen years of a self-imposed prison were finally at an end.

I immediately lit a lamp and put it outside of the door signaling that I needed a midnight messenger. Seeing this, Dustin dropped several items on the kitchen table and left through the front door. When the messenger arrived, I sent a message to my mother to let her know that we were coming and to prepare space for us.

As I sat on a chair in my bedroom, I was completely shocked. I had not heard anything from Dustin about this issue for over four years. I had assumed that it was over, and that I did not have to deal with it anymore. Never had he mentioned that he had issues with looking at little girls since his sister! Looking at women was bad enough!

I felt devastated. I had enough. I could not believe that he had lied to me this long. I realized that this had put our children in danger. "I am not going to have them go through some huge investigation because of his stupid choices!" I said to myself. "They do not have to go through that." I determined to leave as soon as possible.

Some of my friends in the village must have seen my messenger light and that a messenger had come and gone. There was a knock at the door. Kal, the father of a couple of the kids that I took care of stood on the porch. I felt nervous about being alone with him at such a late and dark hour, but I could see the genuine concern on his face. I was concerned what it could look like, or what others might think if they saw that he was there. However, he had always been kind to me, and he had never done anything to hurt me. "Come in," I said as I stepped behind the door.

I told him the truth about what had happened, and that I was leaving. "I'm sorry to give you such short notice Kal," I said. "I really have to go so that I can be in a place where I will have support." "Angelica," He whispered quietly, so we didn't wake the children. "I understand. And it is fine. You have to do what you have to do. I really wish you would stay. I would help you. I could take care of you. You do not have to leave. You have a lot of friends here"

I thought about what he was saying. It was true, I had a lot of friends here. I had connected with so many as I began to blossom and come out of my shell. Many of them never even knew how much they had helped me. I had come to love so many of them, but I could not think of that now. I had to think about what was best for the children.

"All of my family is back in my old village" I told him. "I am going to need their help. I cannot take care of the children all alone. I am going to need to find work to provide for them. I need to go where I will have help and support." "I understand," he said.

"At least let me help you prepare for your journey." He said. "I will be back later in the morning to help you." "OK." I said exhausted. After he left, I continued to pack. I felt sad about all that I would have to leave behind. I felt angry that the life that I had known was ending. I felt robbed.

By morning, news of my departure had travelled quickly. One of my friends, Travis, came to the house with money and other gifts from several of my friends to help me make the journey back to my mother's easier. "We all wish you would stay," he said as he hugged me good bye. "We will miss you. Sorry that we couldn't do more than this for you." "You all have done more than enough." I responded, as I watched him walk out the door.

Soon Kal arrived. He helped me get everything together for the kids and gave me supplies that I desperately needed for my trip. Once again, he tried to convince me to stay. "Angelica," he stated. "I really truly care about you, and my kids care about you too. I really wish that you would stay and let me take care of you. You have been like a mother to my children. I know that things could work out if you stayed here."

I felt that it was too much to think about. I did not want to think about starting a new relationship when I had not even legally ended the one that I was leaving yet. While I appreciated the care Kal had for me, and I was flattered, I knew that the timing was wrong. And it scared me to think that he cared enough for me already, to want to care for me and my children. He could tell that I was not going to change my mind. He gave me a hug and then was gone.

It took several days to get there, but the kids and I returned to my mother's village. We were totally and completely exhausted when we arrived. The moment we were inside my mother's hut we all quickly found comfortable places to lay down and fell right to sleep.

I started the process to divorce my husband, and determined to start my life over. After being gone for over six years from my family and friends, a lot had changed. I felt very depressed and lost, but I was determined to make the best of it.

My mother had remarried while I was away. It was clear to me that she was very unhappy. I felt uncomfortable living with her and her new husband, so I struggled living there for a month, and was thrilled when I found a hut of my own.

I tried to make things as normal as I could, but it was hard. A member of the protective council got in contact with me a short while after we arrived. He interviewed the children and me about what had happened in our previous village.

It was then that I learned that while I was busy packing, the children came across an image of a little girl bathing in the lake that their father had drawn. The kids were shocked about what they had learned about their father. They did not tell me that they had found the image at the time because they were concerned for me. They did not want me to become any sadder than I already was. They determined to hold a small council together to determine what to do. They voted and decided to just throw it away. Because they had seen what it was that caused us to leave their father, they wanted me to never have anything to do with him ever again.

Because I no longer lived in the area, I wasn't sure that I should have the divorce take place in my former village. The laws were different, and I wanted the benefit of having my divorce completed in the village where I was living, where I could easily keep track of what was going on as it progressed through the process.

A few months later, my husband arrived in our village. For about a year I tried to work things out with him, but nothing could change what happened.

Nothing took away my feelings of concern for my children, and I knew I could never trust him again. I left my children with family and took a journey back to visit with some of my friends in our former village. I did this to remove myself from the situation I was in and to clear my mind.

While I was there, I knew that the right answer was to move forward with the divorce. I enjoyed spending time with all my friends. I enjoyed attending many different dinners, and they took time to pamper me. I felt refreshed and ready to return to my children, and fight the fight that lay ahead.

In order to afford a place to live, I moved the children and me into space in my brother's hut. It seemed like a good idea, since I had rented to Blaze's fiancé before they married, when times were better for me.

I filed for divorce in our village and fourteen years of marriage came to an end. After a short while, my brother told me that he was going to have a visitor that would be staying for a while. "Angelica, I want you to be a friend to Thomas when he comes. He is traveling from a completely different land and is not going to be familiar with the territory. You are going to need to share your kitchen and living space with him. He will be in a different bedroom, but there are some areas of the hut you will need to share with him."

I fumed on the inside. "How come no one asked me if this is ok with me?!" I questioned myself. I was frustrated and hurt that my feelings and needs had not been considered. I knew that I would feel awkward about sharing my space with a man that I did not know well.

Blaze continued, "He is an older man. He has never been married and he is about nine years older than you." "Great." I thought to myself. "This is the last thing that I need. Some old guy that is going to just get in my way."

The day arrived when I met my brother's visitor. He was not anything like I thought he would be. He looked young, he was strong, and his skin was the color of a dried coconut shell. He had dark black hair that was cut very short that looked wavy on the top. He was close to six feet tall. He smelled like tropical spices, and carried himself with an air of gentleness, meekness and peace.

I was quickly knocked off balance as I looked into his dark chocolate eyes. They exuded love, kindness and a deep spirituality. He smiled as he said, "Hi, my name is Thomas.

www.ingramcontent.com/pod-product-compliance
Lightning Source LLC
Chambersburg PA
CBHW031835170626
46807CB00004B/1466